BEHIND DARK
DOORS (TWO)

SUSAN MAY

ALSO BY SUSAN MAY

NOVELS

The Goodbye Giver (THE TROUBLES KEEPER 2)

(COMING JULY 2019)

Best Seller

The Troubles Keeper

Back Again

Deadly Messengers

NOVELLA

Behind the Fire

291

(COMING FEBRUARY 2019)

OMNIBUS

Happy Nightmares! Thriller Omnibus

SHORT STORY COLLECTIONS

Destination Dark Zone

(COMING MARCH 2019)

Behind Dark Doors (one)

Behind Dark Doors (two)

Behind Dark Doors (three)

Behind Dark Doors (the complete collection)

(Includes one, two and three)

WHISPERSYNC AUDIBLE NARRATION

Best Seller

Back Again

Deadly Messengers

The Troubles Keeper

Behind
Dark Doors
TWO

SIX SUSPENSEFUL
SHORT STORIES

INTERNATIONAL BEST SELLING AUTHOR
SUSAN MAY

BEHIND DARK DOORS (TWO)

Another Six Suspenseful Short Stories with a Twist!

For lovers of Twilight Zone, Black Mirror and Stranger Things

Enter more strange worlds and meet their unusual and terrifying residents. Dive into the **second collection** of **Behind Dark Doors**, filled with stories of suspense, horror, paranormal and supernatural, from the dark mind of short story award-winning author Susan May.

SCENIC ROUTE

When a young family stop overnight at a quaint country bed-and-breakfast what they don't know is that something is wrong in Broken Springs, population 402.

. . .

HIDE-AND-SEEK

Henry doesn't like playing hide-and-seek because his siblings don't play nicely. Until the day he discovers there are worse things than being found. Not being found.

HARASSMENT DAY

Dammit, thinks Edwin, when he sees those people have followed him onto the train and they've even gotten off at his station. What can he do to be rid of them for good?

THE MONSTER RULES

When Harry's best friend shares the Monster Rules he learns how to stay safe at night until he's awoken by strange, scratching noises. Luckily, he knows what to do.

WHERE WE ONCE WERE

Tamara dreamed of visiting her distant ancestors' 1897-time line for her PhD research paper. What she discovers is a family secret two hundred years in the making.

DESPERATE

Two agitated women run into freeway traffic. Both are horrifically injured and should be dead, but they're determined to get to the other side. What awaits them there?

☆☆☆☆☆ "Short stories at their best"

★★★★★ *"5.0 out of 5 stars* It totally lived up to the hype!"

★★★★★ "I absolutely loved this collection!"

This book is dedicated to O'Henry, Edgar Allan Poe, Hans Christian Anderson, Alfred Hitchcock, Jeffrey Archer, Stephen King and every other master of the short story form.
You've inspired me since I was four years old.

WELCOME TO MY WORLD

In the past few decades short stories have become a lost art. When I was growing up in the sixties and seventies they were everywhere; in magazines, anthologies, collections and comics. I cut my reading and writing teeth on them and they've entertained and inspired me ever since.

The stories that most stayed with me, the ones I read over and over again, are all shorts. Stephen King's 1972 *Battleground*, Edgar Allan Poe's *The Tell Tale Heart*, John Wyndham's *Pawley's Peepholes*, *Broken Routine by* Jeffrey Archer and, of course, all the wonderful fairy tales we all read as children, Hans Christian Anderson, Grimm's and so many more. They all spring to mind as I write this foreword.

Let's also not forget the short storytelling form in television, so popular in my youth, such as *Twilight Zone*, *The Outer Limits* and *Night Gallery.* In my view many of these ten to fifteen minute shorts are up there in the great fiction realm. The irony in these tales is what hooks me as much as the plot. This storytelling is where I fell in love with the art of the twist.

In a 1985 *Twilight Zone* story entitled *A Little Peace and Quiet* (similar to an Arthur C. Clarke short story *All The Time in the World*) a harried housewife discovers a gold pendant that stops time. Ultimately she uses the token to pause time just as a nuclear warhead is about to hit their town. The camera pans out leaving her smack bang in the middle of the ultimate dilemma. Does she release time and face the world's end or will she live alone forever? She wished for peace and quiet and received exactly what she wanted.

Exquisite, marvelous irony.

There too is the fun of the short story. We don't even have to know the backstory or the conclusion to enjoy the ride. So often you are left with an unanswered question. In fact, the more ponderous the conclusion the more satisfying the story.

The trick to writing a good short tale is to understand at what point to leap into the story and at what point to leave. Discovering those moments is the part I love most.

For a writer, shorts provide a wonderful way to explore an idea, create a world quickly or solve the nagging itch of a character or plot that won't leave you alone until you've put the words on paper.

My short story writing career began at six and has continued all my life. In 2010, when I approached writing as a serious career it felt natural to begin again by writing short stories alongside my novels and novellas. Very early on I was humbled to have many of my stories win awards and find publication in international and Australian anthologies.

With the rise and rise of eBooks, short stories and novellas are enjoying resurgence in popularity. We don't always have time to plow through a four-hundred-page book but we can always tackle twenty pages of a short story before bed, on the bus or train, or while waiting at the doctor's.

Thank you wonderful reader for joining me here to partake of these story morsels. Even if you don't remember my name, if I've done my job right, you'll remember the twists and the irony in these offerings.

If you do enjoy them please come back for more in the companion collections of *Behind Dark Doors,* to which I will continue to add. From where these darlings came there are plenty more. I have unlimited access to dark doors and, somehow, was fortunate enough to be given the keys.

Take a deep breath and follow me. You're entering my worlds now.

SCENIC ROUTE

When Pam, Michael, and their young sons take the scenic route through Broken Springs, Population 402, they will never know their terrible mistake. Pam's monster migraine has her wondering why they ever had these arguing kids in the first place. Worried about Pam, Michael stops at a quaint bed-and-breakfast where they are welcomed by the delightful elderly proprietors, Bev and Snow Stillwater.

But when Pam awakens the next day, something feels very wrong about the place. She has trouble remembering things—like where they are going for vacation and the names of her children—and

Michael has disappeared. The scenic route through Broken Springs, Population 402, may have done more than extend their trip. It may have changed their lives. Forever.

1

They'd taken the scenic route, but beautiful as it was, it had added an extra two hours to their drive. It was two hours Pam was *ab-so-lute-ly* regretting. At every turn, she felt as if she should be sighing with the pleasure of it, but instead, only tight little moans left her mouth as the dirt road shook and rumbled the car.

The headache—which she now thought of as a needle pushed between her eyes—was relentless. It wasn't helped by the two pre-teen boys arguing in the back seat. If they weren't fighting over who had used the iPad the most, they were fighting over who was smarter or better at soccer or had scored the high score on "Angry Birds." No, wait. That game was last year—this year the fight was over "Minecraft" or that shooting game that was labeled "R" for violent content, but since every other kid had it she was forced to relent.

The children simply couldn't travel together—or at least no sane human should ever travel *with* them. They never stopped arguing. Sometimes Pam felt as if she wanted to lean back, open the door, and shove them both out while the car was still moving.

Her headache superseded all rational thought and emotional control. She turned around to face the boys and, with the last of her energy, said, "If you don't stop arguing, we will stop this car and leave you on the side of the road. Do you understand me? *SHUT UP!*"

Both boys stopped and stared at her. Then they simultaneously erupted in some kind of horribly loud mash-up reply.

"He's had it since we turned off the main road!"

"He lost all my lives last time he used it!"

"You said fifteen minutes, he's had it twenty!"

"It's *my* game. He's always using my stuff!"

These screams were followed by a loud thump, and Cruise lurched forward as his older brother Connor landed a blow to the middle of his back. Then all hell broke loose. It was as though Pam had said nothing as they returned to the pull and push of the iPad between them while spewing every horrible name ever invented by little boys.

Pam turned to Michael and nestled her hand in his lap. He stared ahead, concentrating on the road, seemingly oblivious to the fracas. He reached down and wrapped his hand around hers and smiled.

"It was your idea to bring them."

"I know," she sighed, "but I miss them when they're not with us."

"And you hate them when they are." Michael laughed. "You can't win."

"It's called motherhood."

For a moment Pam's headache disappeared, as her mind drifted back to the years before children—the bliss of zero responsibility. She and Michael had enjoyed three good years of romantic getaway weekends, holidays in exotic countries, sleeping in, and dinner parties with friends. Simple, selfish delights, filling every spare moment with experiences that they now treasured as their time "B.C." *Before children... before chaos... before commotion... before crap everywhere.*

For a decade, Pam's marketing executive career was on a great trajectory: a series of promotions, and bigger things expected. Then the little pregnancy stick returned a double line result. Eight months later Cruise arrived, followed two years later by Connor.

Now their lives revolved around the children: the lords and masters of the house. She loved them to pieces, but sometimes she viewed them—if she was honest, and it filled her with guilt to be this honest—as something akin to intruders.

Pam's reverie was broken by Michael's concerned voice. "Headache any better?"

The reminder brought it back with an agonizing throb. "No, it's becoming a migraine."

Michael glanced over at her, worry etched across his face. "Oh, baby, we need to kill it before it gets going or you'll be days recovering. We want you well for our vacation."

These debilitating migraines had troubled Pam on and off since having the kids. She wondered if it was hormones—or simply parenthood. When they came, they packed a punch, but she could head them off if, at the onset, she took some strong painkillers and rested in a dark room. If not, sometimes she would end up in the hospital on a drip.

"I don't know, honey. If we stop, we won't make it to the resort. It's only a few hours until we arrive. What about the children?"

Michael lifted her hand from his lap and gently shook it. "Your health is more important. You know that. Who cares if we don't get there tonight? What's one night?"

"No, no. I'll be okay. I don't want to disappoint the children." As she spoke, she noticed a sign along the side of the road.

Broken Springs
Population 400

Inside the last zero of "400" was a handwritten two.

"There," said Michael, nodding at the sign. "*Broken Springs. Population 402.* And for tonight, 406."

Pam shook her head.

"I'm not arguing with you, Pam," Michael insisted. "If there's accommodation, we're stopping."

Pam began to nod, but as she dipped her head forward the pain doubled. She wasn't about to argue anymore. The headache had escalated and was now hammering on the front of her skull as if there were a woodpecker in there trying to get out.

"Okay," she said, laying her head against the car window.

*P*am awoke to the sound of gravel crunching under tires, followed by the squeak and bang of opening and closing car doors. She looked out through the dusty windshield and saw Michael and the kids clambering up the steps of a big old country house. Pausing at the top, Michael banged on a wooden door with an oversized black door knocker. White picket posts capped by a blue handrail fenced the wide veranda. Every third post bore a hollow carving of what looked like a child. Each carving appeared to be unique.

Any other time Pam would have appreciated the charm, but her headache had now escalated into a migraine that turned the inside of her head into a throbbing, agonizing mass. Nausea was overwhelming her senses, and it took all her concentration to keep down her lunch.

A woman's voice alongside her husband's in conversation drifted down to her, then Michael and the boys disappeared inside. Minutes later Michael trudged down the stairs with Cruise and Connor bouncing down behind him; with each step their thick brown curls flopped across their foreheads.

Michael hurried to her side and opened her door. Helping her out, he said, "We're in luck. It's a bed-and-breakfast and they have two rooms. It's old, but it'll do. And we're the only guests."

Pam reached for Michael's outstretched hand. Waves of dizziness traveled through her as she felt herself pulled out of the car. As her legs took her weight, she glanced up at steps that swayed disconcertingly as though moved by an earthquake, and wondered if she had the strength to make it to the top.

Pam rested against the hood as Michael yanked their bags out of the trunk. The excited shouts of the children drifted back to her. She turned and watched them disappear around the side of the house, off to explore their home for the night.

She turned away as their voices disappeared and, despite the pounding in her head, still took a moment to take in the beautiful vista. The house was on a hill, and looked out through a grove of trees to a green valley below, dotted with sheep and cows and segmented by white posts. The surroundings were so quiet Pam could hear the distant bleating of the sheep.

If it weren't for the screaming white noise of the migraine, she might've believed she'd died and gone to heaven. Instead, she just felt as if she were dying and on a side trip to hell.

"Pam, you are white as a sheet. Come on, straight to bed for you." Michael dropped the bags, and Pam felt his arm slip around her waist. He half-carried her up the steps, talking the whole way as though conversation would ease her pain.

"Bev and Snow run the place. You'll like Bev. She's making you a cup of cinnamon and spice tea to help you sleep. It's her grandmother's recipe. She guarantees it will cure the worst migraine. Bev also said—"

Pam barely heard Michael's words. Her entire focus was required simply to put one foot in front of the other and get herself to the top of the stairs.

The bedroom was cool and pale yellow. That was all Pam took in before she lay her head down on the crisp white pillow. Closing her eyes was the sweetest bliss.

Somewhere between awake and asleep she heard the bedroom door open. A blurred image of a plump, white-haired woman with smooth pink cheeks—someone like a country Mrs. Claus—leaned over her, pulling her up and forward to a half-sitting position.

Pam wanted to tell the woman to leave her alone, but she had no strength. Then the woman held a cup below Pam's mouth and pressed it to her lips, the whole time making soothing, tutting sounds.

The brew smelled spicy and warm, and yes—there was a cinnamon tang. As she sipped it in, she felt a distinct tingling in the back of her mouth. The feeling quickly moved down her throat, where it turned into an uncomfortable numbness. Just as she began to panic, the sensation was gone, followed by an unexpected, wonderful feeling of peace. She took two extra gulps, and then motioned the woman away.

Her head fell gently back to the comforting pillow. As she fell away into blissful oblivion, the last thing she remembered was the odor of freshly made Christmas cake. The smell took her back to the years before kids—when she had time to bake. When her time belonged only to her. When there was the time to spare—to fuss with Christmas lunch, to sit, to read, to talk to Michael about life, instead of children's needs, and the most wonderful pleasure of all, to sleep.

3

*T*hrough a fog of confusion, Pam opened her eyes. She was in a darkened room cloaked by silence. Instinctively, she rolled over to reach for Michael. He wasn't there. Her hand smoothed along the starched sheets feeling for a warm spot, but the feel of the bedclothes only revealed that she was not in her own bed.

She rolled onto her back and scanned the room. Light filtered through the lace that peeked out from a crack in the blue chintz curtains. In a corner sat a rocking chair, and next to it on the table were their opened bags.

Now she remembered. They were in a bed-and-breakfast. Snatches came back to her. The children running up the side of the house; Michael half-carrying her up the stairs. Something about Bev and Snow. Snow? Was that someone's name? A nickname, maybe? Then Christmas ... the distinct smell of Christmas.

She closed her eyes again and focused on the memory of the migraine. Was it still there? She did a mental check of her usual pain points: middle of the forehead, back of the neck, behind her eyes.

Gone. By some miracle, her migraine was gone.

That woman—she had to be the Bev of "Bev and Snow"—had

given her some kind of tea. She made a mental note to ask for the recipe before they left. Whatever was in it, it was miracle juice.

The migraine had left her feeling drained and weak. Although not as weak as she typically felt. Usually after a monster migraine, she would be recovering in bed for at least a day.

Her skirt and t-shirt were laid across an antique dressing table to the side of the room. She had no recollection of taking them off. Michael must have helped her. Pam gently pushed herself up and out of the bed, even though the urge to just lie there tugged at her like a drug.

She pulled on her clothes and found her sandals at the base of the bed. It wasn't like Michael to be tidy. She was usually the one folding clothes and keeping order. No mean feat when you shared a house with boys. The image of two small faces flashed into her mind, followed by a feeling of frustration at having to constantly clean up after them. Then it was gone.

It was a funny thought; the feeling of frustration was confusing.

She was the most patient person in the world.

As she opened the door to the hall, she noted how bright it was outside the room. Light was streaming toward her from a doorway down the hall. It was clearly the entrance to the kitchen; she glimpsed wood floors, a pine table, a cluttered wood sideboard, and honey-colored chairs.

The sound of a kettle whistling and a female voice happily humming drifted toward her. Pam listened for a moment but didn't recognize the tune. Something about it evoked in her a feeling of melancholy, yet it was strangely comforting, too.

Feeling like a trespasser, she tiptoed down the hallway, her heart beating a little faster. She had no idea how long she had slept or whether by entering the kitchen she was invading the private domain of the proprietors. She wasn't good with strangers, and she wished Michael were by her side.

But, then, he must be with the ... others. She paused at that thought.

The others.

She remembered sitting in the car, and that even despite the migraine, the charm of the house and the beauty of the surrounding countryside was vivid.

It was so beautiful. The others must be having a wonderful time exploring. Michael and the—

She stopped, because for the life of her, she couldn't figure out why that thought had entered her head.

An image slipped into her mind: of children bounding up the side of the house. Chirping voices echoing. Pam couldn't think about that right now. She wanted to find Michael, and she wanted to eat. She was suddenly starving.

From the doorway, the woman's humming rose and fell with a tune that Pam couldn't quite recognize, although it sounded familiar: like a sad version of "Jingle Bells."

Pam staggered a little, still woozy, maybe from hunger or the migraine hangover. Steadying herself against the kitchen doorjamb, she took a few deep breaths. Then she fixed a smile upon her face and made ready to greet her host.

Even before she placed a foot in the room, the humming abruptly stopped and a warm voice called to her. "Morning, Pam, sweetie. How are you feeling this morning?"

Pam moved into the room to be greeted by the back of a small, round woman standing at the stove. It surprised her that the old lady had, without turning around, realized she was there. Her first impression had been right: she *did* look like Mrs. Claus. Pam recognized her as the dispenser of the soothing tea. She made a mental note that later she would ask what was contained in the miracle brew. This was not at all how she usually felt after a migraine.

The "migraine whisperer" turned from a large, bubbling pot, spoon in hand, and smiled at her as though she were a long-lost daughter.

Pam smiled back and realized, as she did, that she suddenly felt truly happy. She didn't know this woman or even this place—Broken

Springs, Population 402—but something about being here made her feel good.

"Surprisingly good, thank you," Pam replied, as she crossed the kitchen toward the woman, her hand outstretched to greet her.

As she did, she noted the warm country feel created by the pots and pans hanging above the kitchen bench and the chintzy china on the oversized sideboard. A teapot and two cups, nestled on a carved wooden tray perched near the center of the pine table, completed the homey picture.

"I'm Pam. Lovely to meet you."

The woman wiped her hands on her apron—white with big strawberries patterned across it (could this place be any quainter?)—and held out her hand to Pam. Their hands met with a gentle shake. Then the woman pulled her in for a warm hug.

"We don't stand on formalities here, sweetheart. Deals are done on a handshake, but special meetings deserve a hug. I'm Bev Stillwater. Of course I know your name. Michael told us all about you over dinner last night."

Pam felt a pang of regret, as if she'd missed something special, and then embarrassment that she'd slept for so long.

"Oh no, I'm sorry. Did I sleep through all yesterday afternoon and straight through the night? I never do that, usually I'm too busy with the…"

Pam paused at the thought that she rarely slept through afternoons even when she was sick, and certainly not past breakfast in the morning. Ever. That was an odd idea. Michael and she often enjoyed their "lazy weekends," especially after entertaining friends. When enjoyable conversation and good wine were involved, it could be two or three in the morning before they got to bed.

"Sweetie, don't you apologize for anything. Why, I don't think I ever saw anyone as pale as you were yesterday. We were so worried about you, you poor darling."

Abruptly Bev turned to the simmering pot, lifted up a spoon, and turned back toward Pam. She held out the spoon. A rich aroma of tender meat and vegetables in broth warmed Pam's nose. The smell alone was good enough to eat. Her saliva glands exploded in hunger. It dawned on her she hadn't eaten since breakfast yesterday.

Pam slurped the juicy taste from the spoon and stood there staring at Bev. She couldn't stop herself from licking her lips like a ravenous dog.

"Oh, my goodness, Bev, that is divine. You are some cook."

Bev smiled and placed the spoon on a small plate on the counter next to the stove.

"Well darling, I thought you needed some good home cooking after what you've been through. So I'm fixing a hearty country meal for dinner."

"Oh Bev, that's so kind of you, but we can't stay another night." Then she added quickly, as she didn't want to insult this woman's hospitality, "We'd love to, but didn't Michael tell you? We've already paid for a booking somewhere else."

Bev's body stiffened, just a little, her mouth tightening ever so slightly. "No, sweetie, he didn't tell us. He did say you were on a week's vacation. So we thought—"

Pam instantly realized she'd offended the woman, taken her by surprise. She felt terrible. A pang of unexpected guilt hit her. Guilt wasn't something she often indulged. She had such disdain for "guilt-meisters" like those women at work who were always complaining they should be home with their children.

In fact, she'd often say "I'll take a guilt trip when I'm dead; life's too short." Michael laughed every time she said it, often calling her his "little, selfish beauty."

Suddenly it occurred to her, lately, she'd been feeling guilty a lot. She couldn't remember why, and she couldn't remember when it started. There was just an all-pervading sense that this was a reoccurring feeling.

She felt Bev staring at her, waiting for an answer.

"Yes, yes ... we're on vacation, but we were heading to ... um ... to—"

She stopped.

For heaven's sake, she thought. *What is going on?*

Hard as she tried, she couldn't remember where they were going. She wanted to say "a resort." Then why would they head for a resort? They weren't resort people. They were cozy roaring wood-fire cabin people; or luxury beachside Mai Tai bungalow people. Resorts were filled with too many people—and worse, too many families.

Bev appeared to lose interest in waiting for Pam's answer and began busying herself with wiping down the side bench with a muslin cloth.

As Pam continued to search for words, Bev suddenly stopped her cleaning as though an urgent thought had occurred to her. She put down the cloth and turned back to Pam. In her hands, she now held a tray. It was decorated with an ancient-looking picture of peaches, plums, and apples and held the most delicious-smelling cookies. Her taste buds went wild doing the hokey pokey in her mouth.

Pam smelled the same Christmas-cake scent wafting from them she'd noticed the day before in the tea. What *was* that aroma? In her entire life, she was sure nothing had ever smelled this wonderful.

It was orange and lemony, ginger and sugar, and something extra, something, something warm and familiar and comforting that reminded her of childhood, and the smell of spring and rain, and running through the forest, and candy canes and, and... something else important she couldn't remember.

Ahh, it was driving her crazy. The thing was just at the edge of her memory.

She just had to have a cookie. Before she had time to think about it, she had scooped up two of the warm golden circles, suddenly not caring if she appeared greedy or rude—which just wasn't like her.

Manners were necessary. Manners reflected your upbringing. She'd told Michael that many times. No, not Michael ... she hadn't told Michael to "mind his manners." She didn't need to reprimand him.

So if not Michael, whom did she tell? An intense vision of her repeatedly scolding someone floated through her mind. As she tried to think about it, little knots of frustration grew in her stomach. Though she couldn't remember who it was, she just *knew* they never listened. For some strange reason it really mattered to her they listen and learn. Why she cared they "listened and learned" she didn't know, because she was the most easygoing person you could ever meet.

She tried out the idea again; the object of her lecturing was Michael. That just didn't feel right. He was a real gentleman. He always opened the car door for her, without fail. That courtesy alone made her feel like a princess.

Except now, sometimes, she opened the car door for herself.

When? When did she start opening her own door?

The car. Something about the car, and why he didn't open it. Now it was coming to her.

She was remembering there was always something to pick up and remove from the car: carry bags, and sweaters, and trash—so much trash—especially from the back seat. Images flashed through her mind: sweet faces smiling at her, small hands clutching a toy, a spilled drink, a singsong tune repeated constantly, dirty handprints on the headrest.

Then the images were gone, and she was left with the only conclusion, which made sense: Michael was taking her for granted. The two of them needed to sit down and have a good long talk. There was no way she would allow their marriage to go down the path of *we've been together long enough I don't need to try anymore.*

As Pam crunched on a cookie—which tasted even better than it smelled, if that was even possible—she felt the same tingling, prickling numb feeling in the back of her throat she had felt when drinking the tea. Then a second later it was gone, and she was consumed by the delicious buttery sensations in her mouth.

"Mmm, mmm, Bev—you are a genius in the kitchen. You should have your own bakery business."

A smile traveled across Bev's face, from her mouth to her bright gray-blue eyes. She looked almost backlit. Pam glanced above and behind the woman to see if a small window was casting the gentle light. There was nothing there. The light appeared to be coming from the woman herself. Then Bev opened her mouth to speak, and it was gone.

"Why, sweet pea, you are just darling." Bev patted Pam's arm. "But we already have a business."

"Oh, you're farmers, aren't you? That's what people do out here in this gorgeous country."

"Oh no, honey. That's not us. Snow and I were put on this earth for bigger things than farming. We're here to look after good folk passing by, like you."

Bev paused, catching her breath, as her smile transformed into a dreamy contented look—as though she were thinking about something so pleasurable it filled her to the brim with joy.

"We get a thrill out of knowing folks leave here and travel on a touch lighter, with a little less stress in their lives. Sure makes us proud that we've done our modest bit."

Wow, Pam thought *I'm really in Countryville.* Nobody thought like that in the city. Most people there seemed far happier to add buckets of stress *into* your life. In fact, occasionally Pam and Michael had played with the idea of moving out to the countryside for that very reason.

It wasn't a serious discussion, but every now and then when the myriad of annoying little frustrations peppering their lives built up too much, they pondered living somewhere where people thought and acted just like this woman. They wouldn't, because the schools weren't as good.

Hang on, she thought. *As if schools are a priority!* No, it was the *jobs* weren't as good. Not the schools ... the *jobs*!

They would never do it, move, that is. It was just a conversational game. She stood there looking at Bev's sweet smile, breathing in the Christmas-cookie smell and marveling at the memory of how good that beef stew tasted. It made Pam wonder why they didn't start taking that conversation a little more seriously.

In the back of her mind, she knew there were a couple of very good reasons why they couldn't—wouldn't—move, but like everything else today she just couldn't think of them.

Shoving the last cookie into her mouth, it dawned on Pam, as much as she wanted to stay, they really needed to leave. Bev held up the tray again and offered another cookie. Pam shook her head.

"Bev, I'm wondering, where is my husband? We probably should get going." Quickly she added, "Much as we *really* don't want to leave."

"No, no, of course, darling. Don't you fuss about moving on. We don't expect folks to stay forever. Much as we'd love it. You've done your bit, we've done ours, and that's how it's meant to be."

She blessed Pam with a motherly smile. "Oh, and your lovely young man is out back, helping Snow chop wood. Michael's already had his cup of tea."

Michael, chopping wood? Pam raised her eyebrows. Now *that* was something to see. They'd always paid to have their wood delivered—and pre-chopped. "Cheaper for us to pay someone," Michael would say. "Our time is valuable."

They didn't light the fire as much lately, but the thought of chopped wood reminded her how romantic it was to eat dinner on the floor, picnic-style, before the gently flickering flames. A home-cooked four-course Indian meal, a bottle of quality red, and the fire. It was their Saturday evening routine until ... until ...*when did they stop doing that?* More to the point, why?

Pam was suffused with a sudden determination. She would ensure after this trip they'd resurrect these rituals, which seemed to have fallen by the wayside. If they weren't careful, before they knew it Michael wouldn't be brushing his teeth every day, and she would skip combing her hair. From there it was a quick downward slide to complacency.

It was lucky she'd seen the path they were on before they'd gone too far. Thank goodness they had this week's vacation to begin rebuilding the fundamentals of their relationship.

As she skipped out the door in search of her husband, she wore a satisfied smile.

What a stroke of luck we took the scenic route and came upon Broken Springs, Population 402.

4

*F*ollowing Bev's directions, Pam navigated her way down the back stairs to a pathway alongside the house. From there, she followed a short tree-lined track up a small hill situated at the back of the house.

The surrounding trappings of a country life charmed her: a push mower; a vegetable patch with sprouting, bushy, green plants; trees heavy with fruit—oranges, mandarins, lemons; and even a white archway laced with a tangle of roses.

She breathed in deeply, enjoying the freshness of the unpolluted air, and thought, *this is the life*. Several steps later, she found herself breathing deeply for a whole other reason. Her thighs began to burn with the exertion of scaling the hill. Surprisingly, even her heart rate had dramatically increased.

Odd. Pam prided herself on maintaining her weight and her fitness. This hill should have presented little challenge. Once she was back home she would need to discuss upping her workout with her trainer. She must not have been getting enough exercise. *When had that slipped?*

Up ahead, between the foliage, she spied the mottled-gray and burnished-red tin roof of a wooden shed. The size of a large garage, the shed looked self-made, the work of a handyman of yesteryear. An axe leaned against the side of the shed, and nearby lay a large pile of freshly chopped wood surrounded by splintered wood-chips. The boys *had* been busy.

There was no sight or sound of Michael or Snow.

Pam stopped near the woodpile to catch her breath. She leaned forward with one hand on her knee, the other pushed into her right side to ease a stitch. She really was horribly out of shape.

Scanning the heavily forested area, she was about to call out to Michael when Bev's words suddenly hit her, as though her mind had encountered a fault and required a second perusal before filing them away.

"You've done your bit and we've done ours."

She looked at the words in her mind's eye. They struck her as not quite right. In fact, they struck her—just like everything else had today—as a little off-center.

Maybe it was the migraine. After receding, Pam's migraines tended to knock her out of her mind for a couple of days. Usually, though, they left her with a sluggish *my-head-is-too-heavy* feeling, accompanied by what felt like the world's worst hangover. Since she'd woken up, there had been none of those feelings. She actually felt fantastic—apart from the drop in her fitness level. So why was her memory being so... so faulty, to the point where she couldn't even remember where they were vacationing?

When Bev had said *"We've done ours,"* Pam had understood the lovely old thing to be referring to their hospitality. Bev and Snow had provided a bed and dinner—and good company, apparently—and breakfast for Michael.

Thanks to her headache, Pam had missed out on most of this charming hospitality. Once they got where they were going, Michael could take her out to a romantic dinner to make it up to her.

The *"you've done your bit"* part still didn't make sense. Unless she'd missed something while she slept, or misheard part of her conversation with Bev, or maybe forgotten something Bev had said to her before she'd passed out? She had been in a lot of pain when they arrived.

These memory lapses were a concern. She wouldn't say anything about it to Michael just yet. He always over-worried. The first thing on her agenda was mending their relationship—which, without her even realizing, had somehow begun to deteriorate

Then it came to her.

"You've done your bit. It's how it's meant to be."

Of course. How obvious. Now she understood. Bev must have been referring to the payment for the night. Michael would have explained they couldn't stay, that they needed to leave. Pam wondered why Bev had pretended not to know. It was just like Michael to pay the bill and be organized; he took care of most things money related, even though they had separate checking accounts. She took care of running the house and the... ah, something else was *her* job. Something important. Damn, this was infuriating.

Except ... she did recollect something about a joint checking account. Yes, now she thought about it, she distinctly remembered using it: writing the actual checks and seeing both their names on the bottom of the slip. When did they organize that account? She just couldn't say, as though there were a big black hole in the canvas of her memory.

The sound of laughter drew her attention to the shed and away from the confusion in her head. By now she'd recovered her breath, and was back to feeling wonderful, amazingly fantastic. More laughter erupted and she thought she detected the muffled sound of her husband's voice. Her eagerness to find Michael and tell him how much better she felt had her skipping to the darkened entrance of the shed.

The double wooden doorway was wide, taking up half the side of the building. One of the doors stood ajar. Long beams of wood diagonally crisscrossed it. Planks of wood were piled to the left of the door, as though the building were an ongoing project. Male voices and laughter came from inside.

Pam recognized Michael's laugh, and a sudden rush of relief overcame her. It was something familiar—something not part of this house, or Bev and Snow, or Broken Springs, Population 402. That sound was something from before this trip, before they'd taken the scenic route to ... to— A quick flicker of a resort hotel sprang into her mind, then vanished.

Oh well, she would ask Michael when she saw him. She'd be careful though, because she didn't want to alert him to her silly memory problem. They'd traveled so much, she'd just gotten it muddled in her head, that's all. Her memory surely would be cured with a good rest.

The interior of the shed was lit by a single electric bulb, dangling by a long cord from a lofty ceiling. As Pam entered, she immediately spied Michael and Snow—they were standing at a long bench laden with slim pieces of wood in various sizes. It was obvious how Snow, who looked to be in his seventies, had earned his name: a shock of white hair as thick as a teenager's sprouted like a bush from his head.

"Well, here you are," she said, walking toward the men. Both looked up from studying something Snow held in his hand. Michael greeted her with a grin and moved quickly to meet her halfway, wrapping his arms about her and kissing her forehead.

"Babe, you look so much better. I was worried."

Michael looked from his wife to the elderly man. "Sweetheart, this is Snow. Snow, this is my wife, Pam."

Snow nodded. "Pleased to meet you, Pam. Michael told us all about you at dinner."

Funny, Pam thought, *that's exactly what Bev said.*

"Don't believe a word from him," she said, playfully shoving her husband. "I'm really a very good wife and ..."

Again, she was stopped. She had been going to say something else: something else *she was*, but now she couldn't remember. She was a good wife and a good—

Oh, this *was* getting annoying. Now she couldn't even remember things about herself. *She was a good—*

You've done your bit. The words popped into her mind.

She could remember *those* words. In fact, she couldn't get the line out of her head, or Bev's smile, or the way the old woman's face had drooped when she'd said they were going and not staying for dinner.

Something about Bev's smiling face, and now Snow's smiling face, was really beginning to creep her out. So much so, she experienced a sudden urge to grab Michael's arm, run back to the car and take off for ... for ... *Oh, God, where?*

She looked back at the old man, and in that instant, it seemed to her a shadow passed over him, shading and darkening him, so he became a silhouette and not a person. That image hung there for what seemed liked minutes. Her stomach clenched in sudden terror. Then, just as suddenly as it had arrived, the shadow was gone—as though Snow had stepped out into the sunshine—and he was once again just a sweet, harmless old man.

"It was all good." Snow chuckled.

He carefully put down the bowl as though he were handling glass. "Michael told us all about your wonderful life. He's a lucky man to have a woman like you. He told us everything. How kind and how caring. How beautiful. It's plain to see how much you two love each other."

Pam blushed, and then nervously laughed. "No. Snow, please stop. You're embarrassing me." She looked up at Michael and felt his arm tighten around her waist.

Despite her protests, Snow continued. "Oh, yes. It's lovely to see. Bev and I talked about it last night as we lay in bed. Young love. It's how it's meant to be."

It's how it's meant to be.

The words stung Pam. Why had he said those words, those exact words?

It's how it's meant to be.

Bev had said them about their paying of the account. At least, that's what Pam thought Bev had been talking about.

We've done our bit. You've done your bit. It's how it's meant to be.

Maybe it meant nothing. It could be just a country expression. Maybe the whole town of Broken Springs, Population 402, used those words when describing everything.

Regardless, Pam didn't like it. She was beginning to think there was something missing from this picture. Something very significant. She wanted to tell Snow she knew this wasn't how it was meant to be. That maybe there had been a big mistake. That even though Bev had helped her migraine somehow, and both Bev and Snow had been hospitable and kind, she and Michael should never have taken the scenic route.

Instead, she said, "Snow, you and Bev have been so kind. It was so hospitable of you to allow us to stay when we had no booking, but"— she slid her palm across her stomach and squeezed Michael's hand, which was now resting on her waist—"we really must get going. We've already lost time on our vacation and we have to get going to—"

She glanced sideways at Michael and squeezed his hand again, hoping he'd finish her sentence. Thankfully, he took her cue and added, "Yes, Snow, Pam's right. We really must get going. I can't tell you how much I enjoyed dinner last night, and I appreciate you sharing your woodwork. You truly create masterpieces."

Snow nodded his thanks, and then extended his arms, offering something small and wooden to Michael. "Here. Take this as a memento."

Pam now saw what the two men had been examining when she'd walked in. It was a perfectly turned wooden bowl, created in variegating stripes, from a honey-colored teak to a deep red cedar.

"No, Snow, we couldn't," said Michael, shaking his head.

Snow took a few steps toward them. Pam could see he had a slight limp; his right leg dragged awkwardly.

"Now, now, I insist."

"Let me pay you," replied Michael. "We can't just take it. You've already been so generous."

"Of course you can. Bev will give me hell if I don't give you something to take away with you. Something to *remember* us by. After all, you've done your bit. We're always grateful for that."

You've done your bit. Pam cringed.

That was the moment she remembered something: two boys with curly brown hair—just toddlers, really—running toward her, her bending down to wrap her arms around them. The smell of spring and rain and Christmas. Then the same boys, but older, sitting by the side of a pool and calling to her. Except she couldn't hear what they were saying. It was muffled and distant, as though they were speaking through a glass wall. Then, for the briefest moment, she saw the two boys in the back of their car. She was shouting at them. Feelings of frustration and anger burned through her. Pam couldn't work out why she was shouting or angry. She liked children.

Then the image of the boys was gone—leaving behind a single thought. A memory. Finally.

Hallelujah! Praise the God of memory!

Relief rushed through her. Suddenly she remembered.

She knew where she and Michael were headed for vacation.

There was a beautiful cabin by the lake in Paterson where they spent a week every winter sitting by the fire, drinking wine, making love, and simply enjoying each other's company. That's where they were going.

Now she really wanted to leave here and get there. Get away from these two old people, who had done nothing wrong. Other than continue to repeat that strange sentence.

We've done our bit. You've done your bit. It's how it's meant to be.

She didn't understand the words. All she understood was it made her feel as though she and Michael were the subject of a private joke.

Pam decided that instant it was time to get out of there. So she walked over to Snow, took the bowl, and gave him her best warm smile as she did so.

"Thank you. Of course, we would love to accept your gift. Now if you will excuse us, we'll just grab our bags and go."

Pam reached for the bowl; its smooth contours fit perfectly in her cupped hands. Snow held it for the briefest moment before releasing. In that moment, his smile turned from a wide, glowing-denture grin to a duplicate of Bev's wilting scowl.

Pam's stomach turned. The world spun about her, blurring to the golden and red-brown colors of the bowl. Snow was still there, solid, glaring at her as though she were an intruder invading his space. Something was wrong with him. The urge to get away from this place surged through Pam like fire.

Pam gave the bowl a tug—felt it come free from his grasp, felt it become hers. As she backed away, she saw the smile return to Snow's face. Once again, he was a sweet, harmless old man with an amazing mane of white hair.

Although the moment with Snow had felt dark and desolate, when she thought about it later, the emotions that followed were somewhat wonderful, kind of freeing, as if a whole new life stretched before her. In a strange way, though she could never explain it, it felt as if this scenic route had changed their life forever.

She was never sure if Snow's shoulders didn't perhaps straighten, just a little. If it wasn't an odd look of satisfaction that crossed his face. It would, also, take her some time to shake the feeling, in that split second, when both their hands held the bowl, there had been a tug-of-war between them—a tug-of-war for something very important. Pam would wonder, until eventually the feeling faded, whether she had actually won or lost.

From time to time Bev and Snow's words would come to her. Sometimes, they would haunt her nights.

It's how it's meant to be.

COME BEHIND THE VELVET CURTAIN

Working with an editor is a necessity. It's another pair of trained eyes on your work, pointing out where you've confused present and past tense, sorting out your noun and verb disagreements (those guys can come to blows), and crossing your commas and dotting your sentence endings.

For me, one of the most important benefits of working with an editor is they call you out on overwriting. It's a tricky thing as a writer to be certain you've given your reader everything they need to understand the story. Stephen King comments in his fantastic book on the craft *On Writing*, that a writer mustn't go meekly to their work. He means don't over-explain everything. Have the courage to say it and leave it for the reader.

Throw in the realization everybody has his or her own taste—for instance, some like everything tied up in a neat bow, while others prefer to ponder a more up-in-air conclusion—and a writer has much to consider.

Case in point: When "Scenic Route" came back from my talented editor at the time, David Gatewood, he strongly urged me to cut the last two chapters and, instead, conclude the story as you have just read it.

I let his comments sit for several months. In between, he and I and another writer, Brian Spangler, co-facilitated a pretty amazing anthology of stories from twelve incredible international indie authors. It's called *From the Indie Side*, and you should check it out. When I came back to "Scenic Route" in February 2014 to go through the edits supplied by David, I realized I agreed with him.

I thought you might enjoy a peek behind the scenes of the process of bringing a story to you, the wonderful reader.

Finally, if you're a writer, hunt high and low for a good editor, but do be picky and find one who understands the difference between creating a polished piece and creating magic. They are to too two totally different things.

Read the two chapters, which ended up on the cutting room floor, and you make up your own mind.

CHAPTER 5 - EDITOR'S CUT

As the car wound its way down the hillside, two little boys, their hands pressed hard against the glass, stared out the barred window. Their parents were below, loading suitcases into their car. They had begun to shout. When that didn't work, they banged on the window. The noise was loud and harsh, but still their parents didn't hear. The boys' palms were now red and sore and throbbing.

They had searched around the room for something to smash against the glass, but the room contained nothing except two dirty, well-used mattresses on the dusty floor.

Now exhausted, all they could do was press their foreheads against the cool barrier, tears snaking crookedly down their faces and big droplets of snot hanging from their noses.

The eldest boy reached across to his younger brother and wiped his face, catching the wetness in his palm, which he then wiped down the front of his shirt. His mother would have scolded him for this. But she wasn't there to scold him. She was driving away with their father. Leaving them behind.

"Don't cry. They'll come back," he said, nestling his arm around his brother's shoulders.

"Why would they leave us?" said the younger boy, wiping dribble from his chin.

"Because they've done their bit," came a voice from behind them. It was the ancient, creepy lady, who'd brought them food since yesterday. They'd been so captured by the sight of their departing parents they hadn't heard the door open. "Now, it's your turn to do yours. That's how it's meant to be."

"We don't understand," said the older boy, eyes red and pleading. "Why would our parents leave us? What do we have to do? What's our bit?" His voice choked with sobs. "We'll be good. We promise. Please call them and tell them to... to... to come back."

"Oh, they'll never come back, son. Get that out of your head right away. In all my years, not one of them has ever come back. In fact, they never remember. If they ever do remember you, well, then they just don't remember *us*. That's Ma's recipe for you. Never fails."

The boys looked at each other, unable to fully understand their situation. One thing they did understand: something was very wrong with this woman, this place.

As she stood there smiling at them like they were pretty Christmas tree ornaments, a darkness came over her, as though the sun had disappeared behind a cloud, turning her into a shadow. In the same darkening moment, they realized another thing: her smile was gone.

Now the woman spoke to them quietly and gently, because she wanted them to stay calm. The end was easier that way. She told them a fairy tale about two good witches who lived in a beautiful wood, granting children all their wishes. How later, the boys would sip lovely tea and nod off to sleep. When they woke up, they could wish for anything they wanted. If they were really, really well behaved and didn't scream, the good witch would even give them candy.

Then she explained to them how the witches always did their bit, and the children always did theirs, and that's how it was meant to be.

CHAPTER 6

*P*am stared absently out the car window, soaking in the beautiful wooded countryside. She thought back to the old couple. Even now, she could still smell *that* cinnamon tea. She'd forgotten to ask the woman for the recipe, and a little pang of regret seeped into her happiness. The woman—she tried to think of her name, but it was gone—had been very kind.

She looked down at the wooden bowl in her lap, delighting in the smooth feel of it as her fingertips ran around its edge. She thought how nice the husband was, too. *What was his name?*Something related to cold, maybe. Hard as she tried, she couldn't find the name anywhere in her mind.

Oh well, it didn't matter. It was just an old house on a scenic route.

Reaching her arm across the gap between her and Michael, she settled her hand into his lap, looked across to him and smiled. Her head filled with thoughts of the lovely week ahead. It crossed her mind if they'd had children, like all their friends, they wouldn't be able to sneak away like this and enjoy being together.

Just then she noticed the sign—the same one they'd seen when they'd entered the town. Except now it had changed.

Broken Springs. Population 404.

Now a four had been written inside the last zero.

"That's funny," she said to Michael. "I'm sure that sign read 402 on the way in."

"Really? Someone must have had twins overnight."

"Yes, maybe."

Then, when she looked again, Pam saw she was mistaken. Now it was clear the number was 402.

She could have sworn the two had just been a four. A strange churning feeling began in her stomach and then abruptly disappeared, replaced by a calm, euphoric sensation.

"Never mind, my mistake. That headache must have fried my brain. It still says population 402."

Then she added, although she didn't know why, "That's how it's meant to be."

FROM THE IMAGINATION VAULT

We were on holidays in the beautiful scenic wine-country area of The Hunter Valley in New South Wales, Australia. It *should* have been a wonderful car journey to arrive at our isolated cottage for our vacation.

There was one problem. I had the most excruciating headache, bordering on a migraine. By the time we arrived at the house; I had my coat over my head, and I am told I was moaning something about seeing white light.

Several days later, still a little groggy, I joined my family on a sightseeing drive. We drove past a quaint little farmhouse on a hill. For the briefest moment, I registered a sign outside the house with the names of the owners, "Snow and Bev" and a surname. Instantly, it occurred to me these were great names for characters.

On the same drive, the kids were in the back seat fighting, as usual, and driving us crazy. By the time we arrived home the set up for the story was there.

What I didn't know when I began writing was what would happen in the story and what type of creatures Bev and Snow were. While I was writing the story, I actually thought they were vampires. In the end I will leave it up to you to decide what the story is really about. Are Bev and Snow witches or vampires? Is Pam crazy? Is she dreaming? Does she really have children to lose?

There's one thing I am left with, and that's the knowledge it is not always the best idea to take the scenic route. You never know what's down that detour.

HIDE-AND-SEEK

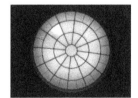

Henry doesn't like playing hide-and-seek. His brother and sister always find him. When they do, nasty things happen. That is, until the day Henry discovers the perfect hiding spot, where he discovers there are worse things than being found. Not being found.

HIDE-AND-SEEK

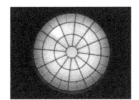

They were looking for him. Henry's heart thumped as he squeezed his eyes shut and held his breath, silently counting.

From somewhere downstairs came the frightening sounds of cupboards being opened, chairs being moved, and doors being slammed.

One. Two. Three … Nine. Ten. Eleven—

He stopped at eleven because he couldn't remember what came next. He'd learned numbers at school, but he wasn't very good at them. Mrs. Walsh had said—through tightened lips that made her look like a goldfish—"Henry, if you weren't off with the fairies you might remember a few more things."

Clarissa and Parker's favorite pastime was hide-and-seek, but Henry hated the game. He wished he *were* off with the fairies. He counted while he waited for them to find him, because it took his mind off his fear.

Small popping sounds erupted from his mouth with each breath. He tried to stop making the noise, but being frightened always made it happen. Once he'd even wet his pants, which only made matters worse. His siblings laughed even more as they pointed at his crotch while dancing about him.

Slowly he eased open his eyes. Except for a small slit of light that shone beneath the door, he was immersed in blackness, so black it seemed to drain most of the air from the closet.

Henry bent his head to his chest, pulled his legs closer in to his body, and wrapped his arms more firmly about his knees. He imagined himself a tiny ball; he figured the smaller he became, the harder he was to find. If he wished hard enough, maybe he'd disappear entirely. Just like a genie.

But they *always* found him. Then they'd drag him out of his hiding place and throw him into the center of the room. He felt like a rag doll.

Parker, at ten, was bigger than Clarissa, even though she was two years older. Still, Clarissa was the leader. Henry thought of her as the wicked Queen from *Snow White*. She was kind and sweet when his parents were there, but the minute they turned their backs it was as if she grew claws.

They would call him names like "Spinning Stupid," and "Dimwit Darling," then laugh as if the names were the funniest things in the world.

"We're laughing *with* you," Clarissa often said.

Henry never laughed, and he never understood why they did.

They would push him and spin him around, clutching at his body until he became dizzy and confused. It would only stop when he fell over and stumbled about, waving his arms before him in a mad attempt to steady himself.

Though the hurt was bad—often he'd find black and blue marks on his skin—the shame of failing at such a simple task as hiding was an even greater pain and embarrassment.

The crying was terrible, too.

He would cry while hiding, knowing his fate. He would cry when they found him; he would cry when they hurt him, even though crying only seemed to encourage them. It was hard for him to prevent the tears.

"Cry-baby loser. Boogeyman will choose you," they'd then sing as they danced about him.

Occasionally his mother would hear and, in her cross voice, scold them. "You two, leave him alone. Look after your baby brother."

While his mother was there, they'd apologize, and cuddle him until she left the room. Then the pinching and pushing started again. In frightening voices, they would tell him tales of the crybaby boogeyman who came for children who cried.

"The crying brings him. He senses your weakness—an easy meal," said Clarissa, with eyes wide and her hands raised, claw-like, above her head.

"Yes, yes," added Parker. "Weak children's flesh is soft and juicy."

Clarissa chimed in. "If he catches you, he'll take you back to his lair and eat you. Slowly. Bit by bit. First your body, and then your head, so you feel every bite. Until he gobbles down your brain." Then Clarissa and Parker made munching noises and pretended to eat each other's arms.

The specter of a monster eating him alive made Henry cry even more. In case the crybaby boogeyman might hear him, he hoisted up his shirt and cried into it to muffle the sound. The more he cried, the more they laughed.

Henry decided when he turned six he would tell them his days of playing hide-and-seek were over; that he was too old to play.

He let out a long breath and listened. In the distance, he heard Clarissa and Parker searching, but the sounds were moving farther away.

Should he make a run for a new hiding place? This cupboard *was* untested. There were so many rooms, and he was always so panicked he never found very good spots.

No matter where he hid, they would probably still find him, he decided. A new place wasn't what he needed. Bravery was what he needed... and to stop crying when they found him.

He wasn't sure how long he'd sat in the cupboard, but the floor felt colder and harder. Little aches nagged at the cheeks of his bottom, and his arms and legs were beginning to complain. Stretching his arms above his head, he angled them back, pushing his palms flat against the smooth wall behind, his muscles grateful for the stretch.

As his hands slid across the wall, he felt something. It was a raised ridge in the otherwise smooth interior. With his fingers, he followed the straight line. It ran for at least a foot, until it made a right angle turn and headed down to the floor. In his mind, he saw the outline as if his fingers had eyes.

With a bit of wriggling, Henry turned himself around so he now kneeled before the wall. Placing his palm on the panel, he pushed his hand along the surface. It felt rough, like the old wooden fence down past the pond. The line, which now felt more like a crack, was as tall as him and as wide as the distance of his outstretched arms. The line ran down the other side, too. To his mind, it made a square, just like they'd learned at school.

A door? That's what it felt like.

How could there be a door here, though, he wondered? This was the last room on this side of the house. Unless... unless it was the door to a secret room.

A secret room would be brilliant, and it would make the perfect hiding place, he thought, excited at his discovery. He ran his hand all over the interior of the outline, but could find no doorknob. If he only had a flashlight, it would make things so much easier. Fingers were terrible for looking.

He could open the closet door and let in some light, but that was a risk. Clarissa and Parker might be anywhere; for all he knew they were right outside the cupboard, just waiting to pounce.

If he was ever caught not trying to hide, they delivered a "flicking" with a wet towel. Flickings hurt so bad. They always made him cry. He shivered at the thought of the crybaby boogeyman.

The more he felt the wall, though, the more certain he was it was a door, even if it had no door knob. Perhaps it was like the dog-door in the kitchen, and all he needed to do was push hard against it to make it swing open.

Leaning on one arm, he reached out with the other, and shoved as hard as he could at the bottom of the panel.

Nothing happened.

No movement at all.

Maybe it wasn't a door.

He sat up and felt around the ridge again. It sure felt like a door, and he detected a faint movement of air coming through the crack. Something lay beyond, and the urge to discover the secret was irresistible.

He changed his position, sitting up higher and pushing harder further up. That didn't work either.

Then he had an idea. What if he used his leg muscles just like he did on his swing, and thrust his legs forward as hard as he could?

Henry lowered himself to the floor, so he lay on his back, with his head against the outside closet door. He imagined his muscles powering up just like the cartoon Road Runner as he coiled back his legs. He was about to let fly, when he heard the giggles. He froze.

Clarissa and Parker were near. He stopped breathing so he could listen. Doors creaked open, then slammed shut. A chair scraped across the floor. Running feet. Muffled voices. They were close enough for him to hear Clarissa, in her singsong voice, call out, "Henry! Oh, little crybaby Henry! Where are you?"

Then came the sound of shattering glass, immediately followed by loud, wild laughter. Henry's legs, which were paused in mid-kick, dangled in the air as if he were riding a tricycle that had been suddenly pulled away from him. He couldn't move and he'd run out of air. He exhaled, then dared to draw a deep breath.

More over-loud laughter erupted, a warning of what awaited him when he was found. They'd broken something, but seemed unconcerned, which meant they'd eaten *mischief* for breakfast—his mother's explanation for their naughty moods.

Mischief days were awful, their games taking on an extra level of pain. They might tie his hands behind his back, or a place a bag over his head, or give him a pretend beating for his naughtiness.

"It's not pretend, if it hurts for real," he once protested.

"Of course it's pretend," Clarissa said, pinching his cheek so hard it left a red mark for the rest of the day. "We wouldn't hurt you for real. You're our little crybaby brother."

A little bird of fear fluttered in his chest, and he couldn't hold his breath any longer. His mouth flew open and he gulped in a lungful of the dusty closet air.

He thought again about changing his hiding place. The image of the wet towel flicking gave him incentive. He would run—maybe he could get down the stairs and find his mother before they caught him.

He tried to flip his body over in the confined space, but in his haste, he kicked out with his right leg and connected with the wall. There was a loud click, as he felt the panel give way and his foot push through into empty space.

He'd opened the door!

Quickly Henry wiggled through the opening, sliding on his bottom, and pushing himself along with his hands like an upside down lizard. Once through, the door sprung shut behind him with a loud clap, startling him. He waited a moment to see if they'd heard him, before rolling over onto his belly, and staying there until he caught his breath.

The dust on the floor felt thick and soft like baby powder, but without the sweet, comforting smell. It coated his tongue with grit. A sudden urge to spit and cough rose in him. He clapped his hand over his mouth and counted.

One ... two ... three ... four ...

He told himself if he made it to the forgotten number, then maybe the cough might disappear as if the number had taken on magical powers.

Five ... six ... seven ...

The cough held, caught in his throat.

Eight ... nine ... two deep breaths ...

Ten ... eleven.

He felt his throat tighten as the cough went back down to his lungs. He had stopped it, and to his thinking, saved himself, for as he did, he heard the sound of the door of the main room opening. Instinctively, he wriggled his body further into the space, curling into his best safety-ball position.

As he lay there, he looked around the room. To his left, light filtered through small, scattered holes in the wood-paneled exterior wall. It was enough to reveal he was in a small room—what type of room, he couldn't tell.

Beyond the closet door, the sounds of Clarissa and Parker searching the room were loud and too near. Any moment now they could open the closet door and discover the entrance to his hiding place. They might even already know about the room.

He heard a click, followed by the closet door's hinges whining as it was yanked open. Then he heard Clarissa's voice, dripping with sweetness.

"Are you in here, Henry boy? Come out. Come out."

His heart jumped into his mouth. Surely Clarissa must hear it beating? It sounded so loud to him... He pushed himself flatter into the floor and into the horrible dust. He didn't care about the dirt or the smell, he just didn't want to be found.

Then Parker spoke, sounding annoyed. "He's not in here, I told you. You always think you know where he is. I say he's in the bath-room, behind the door, as usual ... the stupid little cry-rat."

Clarissa sighed. "If he's not there, I've had enough. I'm bored with looking for him today. I'm going for a ride before it gets dark."

Then the cupboard door slammed shut, and Henry began to breathe again, as the silence settled on him, bringing warm feelings of relief. He'd survived today's game, and he was one day closer to his birthday and no more hide-and-seek.

At the sound of their footsteps receding, he turned his attention back to the room. A little thrill shot through him. He instantly became a brave explorer in a darkened cave, searching for treasure.

His eyes, now adjusted to the muted light, scanned the space around him. The room was long and thin, much smaller than his bedroom, with no windows. The floorboards wooden, not carpeted like all the other rooms and, where the light struggled through the cracks in the wall, there were thousands of dust threads hanging in the air. It couldn't be an attic. They already had one of those; he didn't think houses had two attics, and there was nothing stored here like in the one upstairs.

It must be a secret room, hidden away a long time ago, so long ago it had been forgotten. How exciting to have stumbled upon his very own secret and mysterious place.

Henry climbed to his feet, dusting at his clothes with his hands. He decided to measure the room the way his father measured distances—by watching his feet and counting steps. He moved to the beginning of the opposite wall, then took off down its length, his shoulder brushing along it. At eight steps he came to the end, bumping gently into the wall.

Turning, he followed along this side, again counting as he went.

Ten. Eleven. That number he couldn't remember. Thirteen. Fourteen.

That missing number annoyed him. He fixed his mind on the symbols for eleven and thirteen—and searched for the image of it. *Where was it in his brain?*He was thinking so hard he didn't notice the chair and walked straight into it, falling face first into its dusty, plump cushion.

Dust tickled the back of his throat, and he sneezed. Pushing back from it, he stood up. Then, leaning forward, he ran his hand over one of its arms. The material felt soft and spongy. The chair was bigger than he was, and wide, with oversized patterned cushions, upholstered with pink and red roses entwined with dark green leaves. There were no chairs like this in the house.

Balancing on tiptoe, he turned and plopped himself into it. It felt cozy and warm, like a big, fluffy bath towel wrapped about him.

Henry decided the chair belonged to the secret room, and because it belonged to the room, and the room was his discovery, this was now his chair. It would become his throne, because he was *the king*. There was a crown in his dress-up box, and the next time he came he would bring it with him, along with a flashlight.

Now, as the king of England, his first task was to create rules for his subjects. He imagined them clapping and cheering around him as he took to his throne.

First law: dessert can be eaten all day on Fridays. On Sundays, ice cream would be the only food. He'd think about the other days later.

Second law: Clarissa and Parker may not enter the secret room, his kingdom—punishable by a flicking.

Third law—

Nothing came to him. He was starting to lose interest in making laws, because he felt a little sleepy. This chair was special and magical, and seemed to want him to snuggle in, as if offering a loving embrace. His mind drifted off to cotton candy and hot dogs and the appropriate days they should be eaten. His head felt funny, too, and he couldn't match the days or remember his original laws, as if a hole in his head allowed his thoughts to leak out.

A wonderful tingling crept up from his feet, moved through his legs, and traveled up his body, until every part of him felt filled with warm, soft sand. His head was heavy; his eyes so sleepy they begged him to let them close. Even though he wanted to stay awake and enjoy the chair, he was powerless to stop them closing, and they fluttered shut.

In moments he was asleep. The gas from the leaky valve, that had once fed a heater in the corner, swirled about him. If he could have seen it, he may have thought it was a ghost. A deadly ghost.

His eyes flew open and, startled by the unfamiliar feelings and the dark, his body shot up and out of the chair. Unbalanced and unprepared, he fell to the floor with a loud thud. Wide awake now, he clambered to his feet, managing a few steps before he stopped and rubbed at his eyes.

Everything was black. Where was the little stream of light from the wall that had been there before he fell asleep? He didn't like the dark. He was scared the crybaby boogeyman might be near him.

Maybe his eyes hadn't opened yet? He blinked quickly. No, they *were* open. It had just turned dark.

Stretching out his hands, he walked in the direction of the wall that had earlier fed the light. He knew which way, because it was to the right of the chair. Standing before it, the slightest whisper of a breeze filtered through and touched his face, but the light had gone.

Suddenly he realized what had happened. He'd slept for so long the night had come. Then another thought crowded in. *Dinner!* He might have missed dinner. If he had, then his Mother would be cross, and he didn't want that. His mother was his only protection against Clarissa and Parker, and the crybaby boogeyman. He couldn't have her cross, no matter what.

Henry needed to get out of the room immediately.

He turned his head left and right, gaining his bearings before inching his way in the dark toward the direction of the little trapdoor. The dark and the silence closed in on him. For the first time since he'd found the chair, he felt afraid.

He became aware of a bitter taste in his mouth; the taste similar to a bad almond he once ate. It was horrible, and he wished he had some water to wash it away. He swished saliva about his mouth and swallowed, but still the taste stayed.

As much as he loved his chair, he regretted coming in to the room. He imagined he would be punished for missing dinner, and then Clarissa and Parker would make fun of him for getting into trouble.

Henry wanted to cry, but he didn't dare. The crybaby boogeyman might hear him, and he was all alone and unprotected. He held back the tears, trying as hard as he could to suck them deep inside.

Quickly he fell to his knees and crawled in the direction of the door. It took only a few shuffles forward before his left hand connected with the wall. He sat back on his haunches and felt around the wall for the outline of the door.

There was nothing there.

Was this even the right wall?

Maybe the sleep had confused him? No, he felt certain this *was* the right wall. Feeling suddenly trapped, he started to panic, his breathe coming in short puffs. He couldn't cry. He mustn't cry. *The door had to be here somewhere.*

Inching himself along, one hand on the floor, the other roaming the wall, he frantically searched.

There it was! The tips of two fingers had found the crack. His heart gave a happy skip.

"Hooray," he shouted, sitting back and clapping his hands. *Who cared who heard him now?* In fact, he *hoped* someone heard him.

Now he had to get it open. After several minutes of searching, he realized on this side of the door there was also no doorknob. He would need to kick it open, like before.

First he tried pushing against the door, but it wouldn't budge. It seemed as determined to stop him leaving as it had been in preventing him from entering. This time he didn't waste any more time; he knew to kick it open.

He rolled onto his side and coiled up like a tight spring. Then he counted aloud.

"One. Two. Three."

On three, he thrust both his legs toward the door, holding his breath as he anticipated the jarring of his feet as they connected with the wall.

This time though, he didn't feel his feet connect with the door; instead it seemed to open before he'd even touched it. It was too dark to see, but his legs had seemed to simply go through the opening. He wiggled his body along until his feet met the outer closet door. There was no sound either, but he was too grateful to be out of the room to give it any more thought.

Cool air filtered over him, and he breathed it in, enjoying the freshness of its taste. There was no light in here, either, which puzzled him for a second.

Of course, the cupboard door was closed; beyond that, it must be night. Henry felt proud how smart he had become. It must be because the chair and his new role as king had made him so much wiser.

He wriggled himself through, crawling on his stomach like a baby —a proper baby, not a crybaby. Not once today had he cried, even when Clarissa and Parker almost found him and he was so scared his legs shook.

Now, half-inside the closet space, Henry bent his body to the left. Once through, he flipped over onto his stomach, brought his knees up under him, and stood up. Turning sideways, he pushed against the door, and found it swung open easily, the hinges creaking much more loudly than he remembered.

Henry emerged into the room as if he were an alien tentatively arriving from another world. He closed the door and turned to look around. The moon shone bright through the windows, and he felt relieved to finally see something other than black. Hurrying to the open door that led to the hall, he noticed the room seemed changed, but he couldn't work out what exactly was different.

At the doorway he paused and leaned his head into the hall to listen for Clarissa and Parker. They could be anywhere, waiting to pounce. There was no sound of them, though. In fact, except for the sound of the wind blowing down the hall, there was nothing.

How strange. Mother hated drafts, so windows and doors were always kept closed. Yet the wind had somehow gotten inside.

Brown and yellow leaves rustled past the door, flitting and flying along, blown by the wind. He stood, transfixed by the sounds and images. There was an empty mood to the house, and he didn't like how it made him feel.

The back of Henry's shirt flapped gently against his back. At the same time, he noticed the air had suddenly become chillingly cold, as if the door of a refrigerator had opened behind him. Goosebumps rose on his arms.

Pulling his arms about himself, he wondered what he should do. *The crybaby boogeyman might be on his way, brought by the wind.* He heard no other sounds of people in the house, and that wasn't right. Perhaps he should go back to the closet, or even further, into the secret room. Surely, his mother would come looking for him eventually.

What about the crybaby boogeyman? What if he found him first? Oh dear, oh dear. If only he hadn't fallen asleep.

He turned back into the room, trying to decide what to do. The windows caught his attention immediately—or what was left of them. Every pane of glass was either cracked or broken. He began to count, so he could tell his mother how many were broken, but once he got to the forgotten number, he gave up. There were simply too many.

With each breath he exhaled, a snaking white mist rose from his mouth, and a strange little ache grew in the center of his forehead. He shivered and wrapped his arms about his body.

This was so confusing. It seemed as if he had been transported to a different version of his house while he'd slept. That idea didn't make sense, but neither did the wind, or the leaves, or the broken windows.

He turned back to the hall again, and moved toward the door. The wind still whistled down its length, carrying its passenger leaves. He didn't wait this time, but took off running toward the staircase, his footsteps echoing thumps as he passed by open doors, portals to empty, shadow-filled rooms.

At the top of the large wooden staircase he stared down over the railing. Below him, the formal entrance lay in darkness. The enormous crystal chandelier that normally glowed bright from dusk until dawn, hung across from him, dead and dark as the rest of the lights in the house. Where its crystals usually created dancing colored lights along the walls, it now only formed shadows.

Downward he bounded, two steps at a time, the echo of the sound of his shoes rebounding in the cavernous entrance. Small swirls of leaves flew upward, stirred by his passing.

So many leaves. Had a storm brought them into the house through the broken windows?

He'd missed so much while he was asleep. What more would he find? The bird was back inside his chest, now swooping into his tummy. He couldn't control it. If he didn't find his mother or father soon, he imagined it might burst from his chest.

He made it to the kitchen, normally a light-filled room both day and night, holding wonderful, hunger-inducing smells; now it was a desolate, empty sight. Other than leaves, it was empty of all furniture. No dining table. No chairs. No toaster. No vases of flowers, always perfectly arranged in the center of the table.

Above the sink, there were more broken windows, with the wind blowing through as if it had every right to invade the house. It seemed stronger in here, too, whistling and beating at him like he was the intruder. As he watched, groups of leaves caught in an eddy and were whipped against the wall.

He'd noticed since he'd entered the room only moments before, the sound of the wind had grown from a whistle to an angry moan.

He needed to find his family. He didn't like the wind, or the dark, or being on his own, or the way the house had changed. Now he didn't care if his mother was annoyed about dinner. He just wanted to feel her arms around him and to not be alone.

Henry ran from the kitchen, heading for the sitting room as fast as he could, as if the crybaby boogeyman was right behind, chasing him with arms outstretched and jaws open wide. He'd reached the center of the room before he came to a sliding halt.

This room was empty, just like all the other rooms. Where there were once towering, antique bookshelves there was nothing. The chairs, the piano, the sideboards, mother's ornaments and picture frames so carefully placed on the sideboard and tables... gone.

Just as in the kitchen, in the upstairs bedroom, and in the rest of the house, this room, too, was empty. It was clear, now, his family had disappeared and left him behind. All Henry could think was his mother must be very angry with him.

Like a doll on a music box, he stood in the center of the room, slowly turning, searching for anything familiar or even for a clue telling where they had gone and why. The ceiling-high windows, leading out to the sandstone balcony overlooking the fields, towered before him, making him feel like a little mouse. They, too, were mostly broken. Their once luxurious, cream and black tapestry curtains danced and billowed in the wind, nothing more than tattered shreds with gaping holes.

Through the windows, the moon shone into the room like a giant flashlight, the yellow-white light creating a glowing path along the dark carpet. As Henry watched the ghostly, moving patterns on the floor, he noticed the wind increasing, as if his presence were some encouragement to it. It shrieked through the shattered portals, kicked up the piles of leaves and hurled them into the air before throwing them back to the floor and toward the corners of the room.

Henry worried if he stayed in the room much longer he, too, would be blown into the air or pinned against a wall, held helplessly there by the force. As if the wind had read his mind, a sudden gust hit with enough force to almost topple him. He staggered backward for a moment, then righted himself. This was scary, and it felt dangerous.

Grabbing at his flapping shirt to hold it down, Henry turned his back to the wind. He now faced the enormous, white-marble fireplace, which until he fell asleep had been a place of warmth and comfort. Now, in his imagination, it was a black-holed entrance to the home of a snarling, red-eyed monster. Swaying cobwebs stretched across its hearth, and the mantelpiece glistened and shimmered in the moonlight.

The possibility of the crybaby boogeyman emerging from the hollow seemed very real. Henry began to back away, placing one foot carefully behind the other, too afraid to look away.

Behind him, buffeted by the wind, the double entry doors banged violently against their frames, as if they, too, were attempting escape. Henry used the sound as his guide. In only a few more steps he'd be close enough to the doors to safely turn and run through them.

Two more steps ... one more step ... now turn.

As he began to turn, something white, fluttering at the base of the fireplace, caught his attention, its movement and color such a contrast to the soot-blackened hearth.

He stopped and stared at it.

It seemed to be a piece of paper with one edge stuck beneath a leg of the iron grate. Even though it flapped like a captured moth, he could see there was something written on it.

A message from his mother, perhaps? She often wrote notes. His heart lifted.

Henry desperately wanted to run from the wind and the fireplace, to look for his family, or find somewhere to hide until they came back if he couldn't find them. If this *was* a message, he needed to get it.

Like a waving white hand, the paper beckoned him forward.

He fought his way back against a wind that battered and tore at him as if it didn't want him to reach the paper. Leaves beat at his face, arms, and legs, their sharp edges biting into his skin, but he kept going. Henry held up his hands and covered his face, leaving his fingers slightly parted over his eyes so he could see. Each step took so much more effort than it had taken only minutes before.

At the grate, he bent down and pulled at the paper. It flapped in his hand as if it were a caught fish. Several times he grabbed for it before gaining a grip and yanking it hard. It tore away easily, but left a small piece of the edge wedged under the grate leg.

Henry clutched the paper, as the wind pulled at his prize. In the dim light, he couldn't make out the words, but he decided if he took it to the window he might be able to see something, with the help of the moonlight.

He pushed and struggled against the wind in a battle of determination. The wind his enemy, the moon his friend, as it appeared to glow even brighter as he came nearer to the windows. He still couldn't read or see anything on the page as he tussled with the wind to simply hold on to the paper.

Then Henry had an idea. He dropped to the floor, placing the bottom edge of the paper under his knees, while his hands held the top to keep it flat. The wind now couldn't catch the edges. Although it flicked at his prize, the page remained steady enough for Henry to examine it. He felt proud to have beaten the wind at this challenge.

Now the paper was still, he saw it was a page torn from a newspaper. His father often read the paper on a Sunday morning; sometimes Henry would sit on his lap until he was told he wriggled too much, and to get down. His father must have left it.

What was on the page was the last thing he'd expected.

There at the top was a picture of him sitting behind a cake. The photo was from his fifth birthday last year; he remembered the cake. He had worn his birthday hat and held the toy plane given him by his Grandma.

Below the picture were many words. They were a problem. He couldn't read them, except for a few easy ones he'd learned at school. How he wished he knew more words.

He scanned the page, and was stopped by another picture in the middle. This one he'd never seen before today. It was of his mother, father, Clarissa, and Parker. They looked odd. His mother always told him he must smile in photos. Yet in this picture, his family looked sad, their mouths turned down like upside down "U"s. His father's arm was stretched about his mother's shoulders, and her head lay against his chest. Standing before them, his brother and sister huddled together so close they looked as if they were joined at the waist.

He studied the image. Why were they sad? Why was his picture there? Printed in big black letters at the top of the page were important looking words. What did they say? The words looked very difficult, much harder than he'd learned so far at school.

What didn't help either was the paper seemed determined to escape, the wind playing tug-of-war with him. Henry kept readjusting his legs and hands to keep it flat. Each time he did, he risked losing hold of it. While his hands were occupied, his face was left undefended against leaves whipping past. Their jagged edges flicked and tore at his skin, and he had to fight the desire to reach up and scratch at his face. It itched terribly from their impact.

As he stared at the puzzling letters, his teacher's words popped into his mind. "When you want to read a big word, sound out the letters."

Henry was suddenly excited. That he could do.

He studied each one of the big, black headline letters and silently mouthed them. Repeatedly he tried to make weren't happening in his head. Maybe he needed to say them out loud and listen to them with his ears; this was going to take a long time.

He glanced around the room, checking the doors, the windows, and the fireplace for signs of the crybaby boogeyman. Except for the leaves and moonlight, he seemed alone. He didn't want to be here, but he needed to know what the words said, and why the pictures of him and of his family were in the newspaper.

He turned back to the page and began on the letters.

"Geh. Aa. Ss. Ga ... ss—Gas."

That was the word. Gas!

Yes! It worked. He had the word.

His joy was short-lived. The next word wasn't so simple. No matter how many tries he took, he couldn't work out what it said.

It started with a *ka* sound, but the rest was beyond him. *K.I.L.L.S*

He recognized the letter *I*, but *I* had so many sounds he wasn't sure how he should say it. Eventually, he gave up and went on to the next word.

"Be. Oh. Ye. Be-OY—Boy."

Boy. It said boy.

Mrs. Walsh was right. Sounding out did work.

Now he had Gas ... something ... boy.

The next word was a problem. He sounded it out aloud, his forehead creased in concentration.

"Beh ... Oh ... Da."

The last letter, the *Y*, was tricky. He said it the way the *Y* sounded in boy.

"Bod-ya?"

It didn't sound right, though.

He kept trying, but could only put the first three letters together, and *bod* without the sound of the *Y* didn't make sense. He stared and stared at it, but the word was too difficult.

The next word he wasn't even going to attempt. It looked like a puzzle; after one attempt, he knew he had no chance of working it out.

F.O.U.N.D

A.F.T.E.R. followed it. It presented the same problem. He could get the "*af*" bit but how to say the rest wouldn't come to him. Quickly, he gave up on that one, too.

The next word made Henry laugh. It wasn't a word. It was a number. A special number—in fact, the number he couldn't remember. His heart gave a little skip. Things were starting to go very right for him.

After everything that had gone wrong—falling asleep, missing dinner, getting lost and finding the house deserted and filled with leaves—at least he knew the number. Seeing it printed there on the page jogged his memory, and the name for the number dropped into his mind like a coin dropping into a slot.

Twelve.

He was getting somewhere. The word that followed twelve was easy, because not only was it on the calendar hung on the classroom wall, but also Mrs. Walsh repeated it often.

"Seven days in a week," she would say, pointing to the word every morning.

Days.

See Mrs. Walsh, he thought, I *was* listening and not off with the fairies. It's just my memory isn't there sometimes.

Now he had four words he knew for sure and four he didn't know.

Gas. *Kills.* Boy. Bod-ya. F.O.U.N.D. AFTER *12. Days.*

Gas... something ... boy ... 12 ... days.

No, it was no good. It didn't make sense.

Just then, the wind kicked up a whole other level, the frenzied leaves tearing at his skin, the sound of the wind hurting his ears. After kneeling on the hard floor for so long, his knees ached. Worst of all his heart was pounding in his chest. He didn't like this wind. Didn't like the dark. Didn't like being on his own. He needed to find his family.

The longer he stayed here trying to read the words, the longer it would take him to find his family. If they weren't in the house, maybe they were outside. He'd try to read the words again later; if he found his mother, she could read the paper to him.

Yes. That seemed like a good idea.

He didn't want to lose the paper, though. The wind seemed very determined to tear it from his hand. Or he might even forget and leave it somewhere—he did that sometimes.

Suddenly he had an idea.

Henry stood up, clutching the paper tightly. Then, despite being buffeted even more by the wind, he took great care in folding it in half, being meticulous not to crease either of the pictures. Then he made his way back to the grate, silently congratulating himself for creating a good plan.

So far today he'd done so many things of which he could be proud. He'd discovered the room and worked out how to get inside, found the chair, come up with some fantastic rules as king, and even worked out how to read some of the words in the newspaper. All of this, he'd done on his own, without any help from his brother and sister, or his parents.

He'd been scared, too, but that hadn't stopped him. What a big, brave boy he'd become. He really wished Clarissa and Parker were here, because he might actually tell them to go away when they teased him. Maybe, when he found his siblings, he wouldn't wait until he turned six to tell them he didn't want to play hide-and-seek anymore.

Yes, that's exactly what he would do. He would actually stand up for himself.

The grate was heavy; he struggled to lift the leg still holding the small torn slip. With the chill of the wind, the metal felt hard and slippery, but he was determined. Several attempts later and he'd raised the grate just enough to work the paper under the leg again. He shoved it beneath, holding it there with one hand, while he dropped the leg back down. When he pulled his hands away, his palms were black with soot.

Henry turned once more toward the double doors. After checking a few more rooms, he would then continue his search outside.

His thoughts turned to the strange picture of his family. The looks on their faces made him momentarily sad. He didn't like that feeling. In his mind he changed the image and turned their sad mouths into happy smiles. That's better, he thought.

With the new picture in his mind's eye, he imagined a message sent by his family written under the photos.

Dear Henry,

Mother forgives you for falling asleep and missing dinner. Clarissa and Parker forgive you for crying and not hiding very well. Father doesn't mind you squirm too much on his lap—you can sit there as long as you like.

We are looking for you, and when we find you, we will give you a gigantic hug. (He imagined his mother ruffling his hair, kissing his ear, and whispering she loved him very much. Later, she'd give him the dessert she'd saved—apple pie and ice cream, his favorite.)

Clarissa and Parker want you to know you are the best little brother they could ever have, and they are sorry for calling you a crybaby.

You are a very, smart boy, and we all love you very much.

Love your family

Henry smiled at his make-believe letter. He stood a little taller, his heart a little fuller, as he passed through the doors into the foyer. *Yes, he was a clever boy.*

This was a very good day indeed, because he'd learned he didn't need to be scared of the crybaby boogeyman or Clarissa and Parker. Not only was he smart, he was, also, a very brave boy. Until today, he didn't know that.

No sooner had that thought entered his head, than the wind magically and suddenly died down. The leaves settled back on the floor as if under command, creating a crisp brown and yellow carpet. In the moonlight, it was really quite pretty, and they made a delightful crunch under his feet as he walked through them.

Henry skipped up the hall as a delicious notion alighted upon him, leaving him so excited his heart jumped with joy. He knew exactly what he would do next, and he'd have the best fun doing it.

He would turn the search for his family into a game of hide-and-seek. For all he knew they were already playing; they just hadn't told him. Clarissa and Parker had never allowed him to be the seeker; always, he was the hider.

This time he'd change the rules. When he found his family, he wouldn't call Clarissa and Parker names like they called him. He'd just be happy and exclaim what wonderful hiders they were.

What fun. What delightful fun. Finally it was his turn.

Henry cupped his hands around his mouth.

Then he shouted as loud as he could.

"Ready or not. Heeere I cuuum—"

FROM THE IMAGINATION VAULT

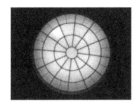

"Hide-and-Seek" began simply as an image of a small, frightened boy hiding in a cupboard. Decades ago, when I studied creative writing, the first story I ever wrote was a ghost story. That story disappeared among the many house moves, and I hadn't written one since.

I do love a creepy ghost story, but the ghost stories I enjoy are not of ghosts rattling chains and slamming doors in an attempt to scare the bejesus out of the living. The most fascinating stories for me are of souls who don't recognize their circumstance and who are seeking answers, just as we search for answers from the beyond.

Poor innocent Henry suffered so with the bullying and then accidentally dying, and that is a sad ending isn't it? What I love about Henry, though, is his indomitable spirit. Even after everything, he turned a bad situation into something positive.

That seems true of so many ghost stories. They force the protagonist and the reader to face the good and bad of human nature, and the circumstances and consequences of that nature. In the end, as much as Henry lost his life, to his mind he won. He got to be the seeker, and for him that was a great reward.

Life and death is all in how you look at it, isn't it?

HARASSMENT DAY

Edwin thought he was spending another lovely afternoon with his daughter and granddaughter. But dammit, *they* had followed him onto the train and they even had the audacity to get off at his station. Now they were on the platform. What could he possibly do to be rid of them?

HARASSMENT DAY

*E*dwin spotted them the moment he stepped off the train. Damn it. They'd followed him.

How? He'd been so careful.

They'd been waiting, watching for him at his station. The stupid buggers jumped on, thinking he hadn't seen them. When the doors slid shut, though, he'd leaped from the carriage. They'd peered at him wide-eyed, staring out the window of the moving train as he waved a satisfied goodbye. He'd caught the next train, and thought he was alone.

Here they were, bold as brass, strutting toward him as if they had every right to be here. What were they planning this time?

He wasn't in the mood today for their childish games. Cassie and his darling granddaughter were meeting him, and he didn't want their day spoiled.

Cassie didn't like them either. She'd often said, "Dad, I'm worried. What if they chase you? At your age, you might hurt yourself."

"I'm all right, love," Edwin replied. "It's my street. I'm not leaving because of them. It's just bad luck they arrived after your mother died —they wouldn't have stood a chance with her."

He'd chuckled at the image of his missus, broom in hand, hounding them. That would have put paid to their games. After he caught one in his bedroom, he'd taken to sleeping with a baseball bat. Today he carried nothing.

Cheeky as sin they were now, on the platform, seemingly confident he was defenseless.

Oh, there's the reason. The cunning big one was here. Edwin had seen him before, giving orders to the others. *It must be his size, 'cause he sure looks dopey.*

Now they were jeering him. Pointing. Mimicking the limp he'd developed after the operation. Their intent was clear. They would harass him, here, in front of Cassie. Ruin his visit. That's when he snapped.

Enough was enough. Instinct kicked in.

Edwin headed right for them. He took off at the fastest pace he could muster, his bad leg wobbling each time he swung it forward. He waved his arms above his head and screamed at them, his face contorting with each shriek.

They didn't run. Instead, they jumped up and down, patting each other's backs and laughing.

Laughing!

Then the worst that could happen, happened: Cassie stepped onto the platform. Her face morphed from a smile into a grimace.

"Dad," she called. "Stop! You'll fall."

Then she was by his side, grasping his arm and leading him away.

Edwin glanced over his shoulder to see them waving goodbye. The big one gestured with his spear. They were only two feet tall but, by God, they were ugly devils, with their dirty animal furs and oversized, hairy feet.

"Did you take your medicine today?" Cassie asked, her eyes reddening.

"Medicine won't get rid of them. Did you see them, Cassie? They're following me everywhere now."

"No Dad, not today. The doctor said there'll be good days and bad."

"Well, today is a bloody bad one—thanks to them."

Edwin turned to give them a rude sign. They were gone.

FROM THE IMAGINATION VAULT

Harassment Day was written for a five-hundred-word flash-fiction competition. The story needed to begin with the first line: *"Edwin spotted them the moment he stepped off the train."*

It is still one of the most difficult stories I've ever written. I must have edited it twenty times or more to get the word count down. How do you create a character, a story arc with a twist, in so few words? A lot of work. That's how.

Years later, I edited it with the help of my editor. It's now snuck up to five hundred and eight words, but I can't bring myself to cut anymore.

I've always liked this story. It's very near and dear to my heart because, believe it or not, it's actually true. That in itself is a great story that is longer than the actual story I wrote. Read on ...

Back in the early eighties, we had a gardener named Jack, recommended to us by a friend. He charged a dollar an hour. Yep, one dollar! The going rate at the time was ten dollars an hour.

He was in his seventies, stocky, and strong as an ox; he'd been a farmer until his retirement ten years before. He would push his lawn-mower almost a mile and half to get to us, also carrying his rake and shears.

Coincidentally, he'd lived for many years, and still did at the time, in the same street as my grandparents—who had died years before I met him—and so he knew them. He always said my nana, Dot, gave my lovely, sweet grandpa *hell*—the women in our family always vocal with our opinions.

The funny thing was we thought we were getting a bargain at a dollar an hour, until we discovered it took him two days to mow the lawn and clean up the garden. He took a two-hour lunch break. In the end, we paid the same as we would any other gardener.

One day I was under the house using the washing machine, and Jack came by and said to me:

"Oh no, you've got them, too."
   "Got what, Jack?"
   "Those cursed little people."
   "Where?" I said, looking around.
   "Standing right next to you," he said, pointing beside me
   I held out my hand to the side at waist height and said, "Here?"
   "No," he said. "Lower, to your knees. There're a couple of them there. The buggers must have followed me."

It was all I could do not to laugh. The serious look on his face told me he wasn't joking. Then he proceeded to share the most amazing stories about these little people.

Apparently, they'd started appearing five years before; they wouldn't leave him alone. They dressed in fur skins, stood about two feet high with wild hair, and would laugh and jeer at him constantly. To me, his description made them sound exactly like trolls.

The males were the main harassers, but the female ones—whom, he said, were incredibly ugly—used to sing terrible songs that drove him nuts. Their diet consisted of potatoes they roasted on sticks around a fire.

Sometimes at night he would be awoken by loud noises in the ceiling. When he climbed up one time to investigate, he said he found a printing press in his roof cavity. They were printing pornography, which they then sold to pay for their food. How did they get the pornography to wherever it was to be sold? In trucks, in the middle of the night—with modified pedals to suit their height.

The poor man had taken to sleeping with a baseball bat under the bed, so if they annoyed him too much he could give one of them a whack on the head, and they would scatter. One ugly, female troll would sit on his bedroom window ledge and constantly wake him at night, until finally he caught her with the bat. After that she left him alone.

He told me he'd even contacted the police and asked them to remove them. The police had come out to investigate, but the terrible things had hidden themselves. He'd even written to his local politician to ask if they could possibly pass a law banning them. Someone must own them, he commented. Whoever did should surely require a license or be made to remove them.

It was quite extraordinary to talk to him. For every question I asked, he would without hesitation have an answer. He was so convincing. I could have talked to him for hours, and I'm sure he would have shared even more endless stories.

I spoke to a psychologist friend about Jack and his little people. He was so lucid in his tales I did start to wonder if I really *did* have little people running around my house and if I didn't need to bring in the pest control. Sadly, she informed me seeing things like this is very common in early dementia.

It's a funny story, but it's also very sad. Jack was a wonderful old soul and a fantastic gardener, and he could certainly tell a tale. He has surely passed on by now, and I hope he's found peace far away from his tormentors.

In my final conversation with him about the little people, I asked him if his wife ever saw them, and what she thought.

His simple answer: "No, she hasn't. She thinks I'm mad."

THE MONSTER RULES

Bailey had survived his eleven years blissfully unaware there really
are creatures just itching to steal him away. When his best friend
shares the *Monster Rules*, Bailey learns how he can stay safe. Until one
hot summer night, he's awoken by strange, scratching noises. Lucky
he knows the *Monster Rules*.

DEDICATION

For my son Bailey, who is braver than anyone I know
and more determined.

THE MONSTER RULES

Serious Warning

This story is a children's story and contains a set of rules. If this story has fallen into your hands and you're a child or an adult who is scared of the dark, be warned. Once you learn the monster rules, you may never again enjoy a peaceful night's sleep. This author was in her late twenties before she dared to break all the rules. Even now, decades later, she is still cautious, especially on windy, dark nights—perfect monster weather.

~

*B*ailey had always believed his parents loved him, his home was safe, and the worst thing in his life was having a smelly, younger brother who teased him constantly about his ears and his love of the Disney channel.

The first time Bailey heard the words "Monster Rules," the one emotion he felt, even more than fear, was confusion. After Caleb explained everything in a whispered, solemn tone, Bailey was left with only one thought: *Parents are liars.*

Unsettling, too, was the story of Caleb's cousin, eight-year-old Ben Stirling, who had disappeared from his home on a Thursday night. Caleb was unclear on the details, but there was one thing of which he was absolutely, one-hundred-percent certain: Ben Stirling had vanished from his bed as if sucked into a black hole.

The culprit was a monster.

"I wouldn't believe me either," Caleb told Bailey. "Except I heard *them* talking about it, and when my brother told me about the monster rules... well, I put two and two together."

"Who was talking about it? Your brother?" asked Bailey.

"No, my mom and auntie—a few weeks after Ben disappeared." A tremor entered Caleb's voice. "First off, my parents have never told me the truth about Ben. They told me nobody knew where he disappeared to, and then later that he'd gone to live with God. That day, I heard my mom clear as anything. She said—"

Caleb leaned in close to Bailey, cupped his hands around his mouth, and whispered, "Ben was taken ... by a monster."

Bailey stared at Caleb, and felt a chill run through him. That was just the beginning. Caleb continued on for the next forty minutes sharing the "monster rules." Bailey's eyes grew wider as he listened, for nobody had ever told him these facts. Not his parents, not the teachers, not a single adult who *supposedly* cared about him.

Instead, they'd all assured him the world was a wonderful, safe place, and all you needed to survive was to look left and right when crossing the road, to always ignore strangers, and to never run with scissors.

What about these dangers he faced every single night? Dangers of which, until Caleb, he'd been blissfully unaware?

Bailey had been terribly betrayed by adults. For no one had bothered to teach him how to prevent an attack by the hideous, terrifying, unknown monsters that stalked children at night in the one place they were meant to feel safest: their own bedrooms.

Caleb was small for a ten-year-old. He blamed it on his aversion to milk, broccoli, and any food in the orange color range. He was big on theatrics and collecting fascinating knowledge. Like the name of the world's tallest man—Sultan Kösen, eight-foot-three—and the largest bubble-gum bubble ever blown—twenty inches. If he wasn't the first person to put up his hand when the teacher asked a question, he was certainly the second.

His hair had a funny way of sitting on his head, as if each morning his mother would take a big pot of glue and stick it down. He told everybody who'd listen the mole on his chin covered a tracking chip his father had had inserted to ensure he would never get lost. Bailey laughed at the story like everyone else, but he did wonder occasionally if it was true, and if there was a risk the same thing could happen to him.

As Caleb went over the rules, he waved his hands with a flourish, like a magician performing a trick. The two boys were huddled beneath the school library stairwell, where the shadows and a thread of breeze provided relief from the midday summer heat. Bailey listened with hesitant amusement that gradually turned to dread as his best friend shared the frightening rules, which would soon take over his life.

"I learned these from my brother, who learned them from his friend, who learned them from his brother, who learned them from... oh, I can't remember. One thing I'll tell you since I learned them—"

Bailey interrupted. "How do you know they work?" It all seemed very Scooby-Doo to him.

"I'm still here, aren't I?" Caleb held out his arms, rotating them back and forth to prove he was unscarred and unharmed. "See? No maul marks. And..." Caleb leaned in even closer, and Bailey noticed how red his lips were. "...on account of my cousin being taken by one of them two years ago. The last thing you want is to be taken by a monster, because they never let you go. That's what my mom and my auntie said."

Caleb's mouth drooped. "My auntie and uncle cried a lot in the beginning—even now they never smile. My mom says every Thursday they *still* lay flowers beneath Ben's window. She says they're sending a message to the monster to bring Ben back."

Bailey shifted uncomfortably. He didn't like this story. It was too close to home—literally.

"Once Mom and I visited at the wrong time, and we caught Uncle Gary and Aunt Mary laying the flowers. Aunt Mary was sobbing into Uncle Gary's shoulder. They just stood there staring at the spot beneath the window. Crying and staring."

Those images—Caleb's aunt and uncle sobbing over flowers; young Ben dragged from his bed—kept Bailey awake for hours that night. How must it feel to be dragged, kicking and screaming, from your bed? If a monster *did* get hold of you, how might you escape?

If Bailey had any doubt about the truth of Caleb's story, by the next week it was gone.

Bailey and Caleb rode to Ben Stirling's house straight after school on a Wednesday afternoon. They stood before what looked like an ordinary house, but in their eyes it had somehow taken on the murky hue of a place tainted by horror. Their bikes lay at their feet, and their school bags had been plopped down and forgotten. Side by side the two boys stood, staring at a small bunch of flowers forlornly propped against the side of the house, below a window that must have opened into Ben's room. Tucked among the flowers' stems and the shiny white bouquet wrapping was a photo of a smiling, freckled boy in a gray school uniform.

"It's terrible," said Caleb. "I really think it's their fault. His parents, I mean. They must have known about the monsters, and they didn't tell him." A stern edge entered his voice. "They're not helping any of us by covering it up. They should leave a warning here, instead of the flowers."

Bailey stared at the flowers, wondering why the Stirlings would keep leaving them when clearly the message wasn't getting through. "What kind of warning?"

"Well, if they cared about the rest of us, they'd leave a sign saying something like: *Ben, taken by a monster. He did not follow the rules.*"

Seeing those flowers was all Bailey needed to finally convince him the monsters and the rules were real. There was another thing he knew, too: he didn't want his parents laying flowers beneath his window any time soon. Or in fact any time ever. So he would follow the rules from now on, and he would follow them well.

He'd had his nightmares. Until now, he'd thought they were just bad dreams, and nothing to do with real life. On those dark nights when he'd wake with images of creatures, claws, and heart-racing chases still clinging to him, his mom would always be there, assuring him with her hand on her heart it was all in his imagination. That monsters didn't exist. She would sit on the edge of the bed, gently stroking his hair, shushing his sobs until he was calm again.

She must have known the truth. His Dad, too. They'd told him often enough they were instructing him on life and preparing him for his future, but never a word about this.

Despite what he knew now, here he was on a hot summer night, struggling to follow the most basic of the rules.

Always keep your arms and legs under the covers, so the monsters can't grab them.

The *tink-tink-tink* whir of the fan reverberated in his head as rivulets of sweat dribbled down his chest and wet patches formed under his arms. Twice his mom had tiptoed into his room to pull down the covers he'd so carefully snuggled to his chin. On each occasion, Bailey had feigned sleep as she carefully folded back the blanket and concertinaed it at the end of his bed.

It was past his bedtime, and he didn't need his mom explaining the lateness of the hour. He also didn't need to defend his need for a blanket on such a hot night. He knew she'd give him the same response she'd given every time he'd broached the subject of the monster rules.

"Bailey," she would say, "there are no such things as monsters. Don't be a silly-billy."

She'd only been gone a few minutes before Bailey leaned down and carefully pulled his bedcovers back up. He was midway through the action when he heard the noise.

Somewhere near his desk, way on the other side of the room, there came a knock. Not a knock as if something had fallen, but more like the sound of a leg or an arm bumping into furniture.

Bailey froze and sucked in a breath. Then quickly he threw himself back with his covers again pulled up. He squeezed his eyes shut and held them closed, feeling the muscles struggle and jump as he attempted his very best impression of death.

In his mind, Caleb's face appeared as a still mask, his eyes closed, as he said: "Look at me. Do I look like I'm sleeping?"

He hadn't *looked* asleep. He'd looked dead. Bailey hadn't known what to say. Then Caleb's lids had flown open as if a switch had been flicked, and he'd narrowed his eyes at Bailey.

"No, I *don't* look asleep. I look dead. Right? That's the most important thing. The trick is to not scrunch your eyes. If you scrunch they'll know you're pretending."

"Why do you want to look dead?"

"Because monsters are dumb. If they think you're dead, they'll leave. If they think you're sleeping, they'll hang around, waiting, hoping you'll make a mistake, maybe move an arm or a leg above the covers. Then *bam*—"

Caleb had clapped his hands loudly in Bailey's face, causing Bailey to jump. His friend had then laughed, throwing his hand against his chest as he continued to chuckle.

"Remember, just concentrate, and you can give a perfectly good *death* impersonation."

Then he'd grabbed Bailey's wrists, dramatically pulling him in.

"Whatever you do, stay *perfectly still*. No scratching, sneezing, or calling out. Don't think calling for your parents will work, either. The monster will have you out of that bed before your parents get within ten steps of your door."

Bailey held his head stiffly as he strained to listen. Time inched slowly by, filled with the clicks and creaks of the house. *How long do I need to play dead?* Caleb hadn't said.

A cloud of doom hung over him. He stretched the muscles in his legs, shuffling his body further under the covers. Surely, the best move would be to get his head totally under and hidden. The less of his body exposed above, the better.

He wished he'd asked Caleb why an uncovered head was safe. Wouldn't it be worse to be dragged from your bed by your head? His heart began jumping. A leg you could live without; a head you need.

As much as Bailey had already slowed his breathing, he worked at slowing it even more. The more he squeezed his body further down the covers, the safer he began to feel.

Thump.

What was that?

Another bump. This one louder.

Thump-ump-ump.

He gasped and then held his breath. The gasp sounded far too loud. Had he been heard?

Now he had another problem. The thumping sound had moved. Or more accurately, the thing *making* the sound had moved. It was no longer near the desk—now it was near his wardrobe. Bailey realized with horror it was now much closer to him.

The freestanding wardrobe was next to the end of his bed, but it stood facing the opposite side of the room. It took forever to convince his mother it needed to be moved.

"Bailey, it's perfectly fine where it is," she'd said. Bailey wouldn't be swayed, though. This monster rule was a very, very important one.

He'd first noticed the lock on his friend's wardrobe on a Saturday afternoon, as the two of them lay on Caleb's bed playing with their iPods. His first thought: *Who would steal your clothes?*

When he asked Caleb about it, Caleb put a finger to his lips—to signal he was sharing a secret—and whispered, "Do you want to know another rule?"

Bailey nodded and stopped playing with his iPod.

Satisfied he'd gained Bailey's full attention, Caleb turned to the wardrobe and fiddled with the lock until it clicked open. The door creaked ajar; the sound it made wouldn't be entirely out of place in a horror movie.

"Keep your wardrobe doors locked and all other doors closed. The monsters can't open them by themselves." Then, to punctuate the message, he slammed the door shut. It made a loud cracking sound, startling Bailey and causing him to drop his iPod. Caleb had mastered the art of giving him a fright.

"If you leave *one* door open... even just a crack... before you know it..." His voice trailed off, as if saying the words would make them happen.

His chest suddenly tight, Bailey mouthed three terrifying words. "They come in?"

Caleb jabbed a finger at Bailey. "Yes. Yes, they do. If you *do* forget —but you-mustn't forget—the first sign a monster's come through will be glowing red spots."

Bailey imagined itchy, red mosquito bites. "Red spots? On me?"

"No, no," said Caleb. "The spots are them: their eyes. They glow in the dark. When they blink, it's like tiny little flashes. It's the light— they can't take it. Not the littlest bit. That's why they come in the night."

After that, Bailey harassed his mother to move his wardrobe as far from his bed as possible. He knew he should keep it facing him, so during the night he could check it. He didn't want the last thing he ever saw to be red, blinking eyes emerging from his wardrobe. Better he be taken by surprise than taken by those eyes.

He wiggled his body back up a little, until just his eyes and the top of his head poked out from under the covers. Beneath the covers, it was hot and stuffy like a steamed-up bathroom. The urge to take a huge gulp of sweet, fresh air was becoming unbearable.

He risked opening his eyes, and quickly glanced around the room, relieved to find no blinking eyes awaited him. Gently twisting his head and wiggling his shoulders, he managed to ease his body up a little more. Now he could peek his nose and mouth out from underneath the covers.

The cool breeze from the fan washed across his face, evaporating the sweat on his forehead, and providing relief from the heat. Slowly —so slowly his chest barely rose—he dragged a deep breath of air into his straining lungs. Then he gently eased the used air back into the room before taking another breath. Air had never smelled or tasted so good.

Did he still look dead?

He felt he'd kept his chest movement to a minimum. His head— he thought his head had moved too much. The wriggling. He couldn't be sure what that looked like from outside the covers. Did he give himself away?

How long do they watch you? A minute? An hour? All night? *Oh brother, what if it's all night?* He couldn't possibly stay like this all night. Of course, the best course of action was to get up and get out of there, to call his mom and dad.

He couldn't do that, though. There was the non-negotiable monster rule Caleb had sworn was right up there in importance:

Never get up in the middle of the night.

"Never go to the bathroom. Don't run for your parents' room. Don't get up for a drink even if you're dying of thirst. Don't even *think* about it," he'd said.

Bailey had been incredulous. "Never? Even when the wardrobe doors are locked and you're sure it's safe and you're desperate to go?"

"*Never-r-r-r!*" said Caleb, the 'r' in never, trailing into the air until he ran out of breath. Then he slowly shook his head, as if even his trailing 'r' hadn't emphasized his meaning enough.

"Imagine this, Bailey... You go to get out of your bed, you're groggy, you're tired, and—what is the second-most-important monster rule?"

Bailey hesitated, wracking his brain. Knowing the rules in order of importance was difficult. They *all* seemed important—*life-and-death* important. Which one was second or third or even tenth, he didn't know; he hadn't paid attention to that detail.

"Come on," Caleb urged. "What must you do to get in and out of bed?"

Bailey thought he remembered. Hesitantly he said, "Never stand next to your bed? In case one is—under your bed?"

"And?" Caleb prodded.

"And, um —" Bailey couldn't think of anything else.

"Bailey, this is important. You've got to jump at least three feet from your bed. Or put a chair next to the bed and jump from there. If there's one under your bed, it can only reach three feet. Just in case they've grown their claws out, then the farther you jump the better."

Caleb grabbed Bailey's arms and squeezed. A tingling erupted in his legs as he imagined the feeling of claws on his skin.

"Thirdly—and this is the scary part, Bailey."

As if the other parts weren't scary enough.

"If the one in the wardrobe doesn't get you because you've been careful not to let your arms or legs hang out, and the one under the bed misses you, you're still not safe because ..."

Because hung in the air between them, and just for a second Bailey wondered if Caleb had made the whole thing up and was secretly laughing at him. No, he seemed deadly serious.

Caleb half-screamed at Bailey. "Because? You're not safe— because? Because, sometimes, *monsters work in pairs.* So even if you follow the rules in your bedroom, another one could be waiting in the bathroom, in the bathtub, just sitting there, drooling quietly in the dark."

∾

Now as he lay in his bed, Bailey wished he hadn't remembered that rule. The minute he thought of a monster lurking in the bathroom, he immediately needed to go. In fact, he was now bursting.

Shhht. Sherrt.

Bailey heard the scratching sound at the very moment he considered breaking the getting-up rule. Instantly, the urge to go vanished. The noise wasn't coming from his desk or even from inside his wardrobe. To his horror, the awful noise—which sounded very much like sharp claws scraping on a handle—was actually coming from the *outside* of the wardrobe. The sound, clear and frighteningly sharp.

Then came a long and loud squeak followed by a click, as if his wardrobe door was being closed. Why would it close the door? To stop the other monsters? That's why. To keep him to itself. His pale, skinny, ten-year-old body was only enough for one monster. That's what Caleb had said—they liked large kids, more of a meal. What about the ones who hunted in pairs?

Oh heck, heck, heck, I know nothing. Absolutely nothing.

The only thing Bailey knew for sure was he'd followed the rules. That this shouldn't be happening. Where was the monster rules expert, Caleb, when Bailey really needed him? Probably sleeping peacefully, safely tucked under his bed covers, closet door firmly locked, and safety chair at his bedside—that's where. And why? Because Caleb was so good at following rules. And Bailey must not be.

The scratching, scraping noise came again. Now there was another sound above the noise—a husky, crackling, wet sound, as if the thing were breathing through a bag of filthy green bog water.

Now it was on the floor. *Yes, definitely on the floor!* It was coming closer, slowly closer, to the bed. Bailey wanted to look, to know for certain what was there, but he couldn't bring himself to face it. Instead, he crushed his eyes shut.

Instantly he knew that was wrong. *Don't squint. Relax.*

Panic moved through his body as if an icy liquid were traveling through his veins. It slithered into his arms and his legs, then into his fingers and toes. Now Bailey was very cold, freezer-cold, with fear.

What had he done wrong? What?

The thought screamed in his mind as he frantically raced through his memory of the evening. He *had* followed the rules, hadn't he? What about when he'd gone down to the basement? Was that when he'd made the mistake?

He'd been sent downstairs, where they kept the spare fridge, to retrieve the ketchup. Yes, he had made a small mistake, but it was only for a moment he'd turned his back on the dark as he was returning up the stairs.

Usually he walked up backward, his heel tentatively searching for the next step. Tonight, halfway from the top, something overcame him. He'd compulsively turned to face upward, bounding up the steps two at a time, clutching the sauce bottle in one hand while grabbing wildly at the rail with the other. With each step, the overwhelming feeling of a cruel black claw alighting upon his shoulder lessened.

Arriving at the top, he'd whipped his head about to stare back down, half-expecting to see the hideous, sharp-toothed jaws of a green, stinking demon descend upon him. Instead, all he saw were darkness and shadows.

As Bailey turned his head to dash quickly through the door and the safety of the brightly lit hall, he thought he saw a flash of red. There was *no way* he was turning back to check. He wasn't *that* crazy.

Sssst. Sssst.

The horrible slithering sound, combined with the complaining floorboards, sounded more and more like a snake. It really could be a snake—they slithered. The scratching before? Cockroaches—they scuttled. The bump? Rats. Big, hairy rats. Creepy and horrible, yes, but snakes, cockroaches and rats weren't monsters. They couldn't eat you or steal you away, or drag you into a deep, black hole.

Bailey wanted to look so bad. He felt his mind willing his head to turn, but he fought the urge. He must follow the rules, because what if it was a monster?

Then he was in trouble. For the rules should have kept him safe would have, instead, done a terrible thing. They would have actually trapped him.

As if he were a pilot doing a pre-flight check, Bailey ran through his pre-bed routine. He examined his movements, counting off the rules on his fingers, moving each digit as he went through his check-list. The main ones, the really important ones, he absolutely knew he'd followed. His undoing must have been one of the less important rules.

Which one, though?

Wear dark pajamas to confuse their poor eyesight. No, he'd ridden his drawer of all brightly colored boxers and cheery patterned pajamas, much to his mother's surprise.

No heat pack or hot water bottle. "They're like mosquitoes attracted to heat," Caleb had warned. It was summer now, and there was nothing hot in his bed. Except him. His body temperature felt set to Furnace.

Leave nothing open.

He was good there. He'd become so obsessive about open doors and windows he'd even checked the door on his money-box safe.

What about the hardest-to-follow rule? The rule even Caleb insisted was a struggle for him. "You might forget to close doors or accidentally wear colored pajamas, but this one rule is an absolute. Even in your sleep, you must do it."

What could be harder than what I've already learned, Bailey had thought when Caleb had said it.

"Have you ever lay in bed on your side with your head pushed into the pillow and heard whump-whump, whump-whump? What do you think that whump-whump is, and why does it keep perfect time?"

Bailey had stifled a giggle. "Of course I've heard it. It's your heart-beat, stupid."

Caleb shook his head. "Uh-uh. That's what they want you to think."

"Who wants me to think?"

"Your parents, you dope."

"It is so your heartbeat. Why would your parents want you to think any different?"

Caleb rolled his eyes. "Ah-ah-ahh. Not a heartbeat, but a beacon. Your parents figure if they tell you, then you'll never go to bed and they won't get their secret parents' time."

"A beacon?"

"A beacon for the monsters. Lying on your side activates it. It transmits your exact position until you lie on your back again. Roll over—and off it goes again. Beeep-beeep. That's how the monsters know you're in bed... and to come for you."

That was the moment when Bailey made a stupid mistake. He started to laugh. Of all the monster rules, this one was the craziest, and Bailey suddenly felt totally silly for believing any of it. He expected Caleb would understand, would actually laugh along with him... but he was wrong.

Caleb went very quiet as he studied Bailey. When he spoke again, there was a tremor in his voice.

"You think... you think I'm lying?"

"I don't know. Look, it all just sounds kind of... well, weird. My parents are pretty on to stuff, and they've never said a word about monster rules."

"Fine," Caleb shot back, folding his arms. "Think what you like. Follow the rules. Don't follow the rules. If something happens, don't come crying to me."

"Well I won't," said Bailey, with a degree of bravado he didn't actually feel.

After that day, Caleb and Bailey had never again spoken of the monster rules. Bailey had always wondered whether, if he hadn't laughed, Caleb would have told him more rules. If there were more rules, then perhaps there was an unknown crack in his defenses.

He'd still followed the rules religiously—even the lying-on-your-back one. In fact, his constant checking of doors had caused his mother to accuse him of having a thing called O.C.D. He'd worked out it probably meant odd child disorder or overly careful disorder, or something like that.

Here he was—possibly because he'd laughed at Caleb—trapped in his own room, under the covers, praying for all he was worth that his mom would come in to check on him just one more time.

Ker-chunk-slap. Ker-chunk-slap.

Oh no! Oh no! Terror was inside him now, clawing at his mind like a wild cat. This sound was close. Too close. Only a few feet away.

There was something in the room. He wasn't imagining it. Now he smelled something, too, like burnt-to-a-cinder meat on a barbecue. It swirled inside his nostrils, sticking there, before it forced itself into his lungs, burning his throat on the way down. A sneeze tickled at the back of his nose; he fought against it. Please don't let me sneeze.

Seconds later, the sneeze receded to wherever sneezes go in the back of your head. Thank you. Thank you, nose.

The rules ran through his head, threads of words hurtling randomly through the gray of his mind. He must have missed one. They'd seemed like scary fun in the daylight but, in the dark, they seemed all too real. All doubts receded when the rotten smell filled his mouth and nose.

Over his face came the sound of breathing: long, strained, gurgling breaths, so close he could feel the gentle movement of the air. The smell wafted over him, hot, thick and rotten—a dirty smell like fresh dog turds. He wanted to gag.

The breath. Oh no! It was on his cheek. In and out. In and out.

Hot. Then not. Then hot again, covering him in a thick blanket of putrid stench that sank into his pores.

He played dead for all he was worth, lying perfectly straight on his back, while his heart sent out the loudest thumping beacon call on the planet.

Eew! Yuk!

Something wet and sticky dripped onto his face. Like slimy glue. Hot and burning. It smelled worse than the breath. It smelled of death. Even though he didn't know what death smelled like, he knew this smell must be pretty close.

Terror seeped from every pore in his body, and every vein pulsed with fear beneath his skin. The horror of it all filled him, until he felt as though he would burst. He wanted to scream. He gulped it back.

The rules. The rules.

He must follow the rules. He could still play dead. That was a plan. This might be a test. A monster test.

The thing was only inches from his face. If he didn't move... if he stayed looking dead... his meat no good... his body too thin... then he might have a chance. It was his one tiny chance to avoid becoming another Ben Stirling. Missing. Taken by a monster.

Stop breathing. Stay still. Play dead. He focused on the words. He prayed. For if he didn't get this right, then very soon he wouldn't need to pretend.

Bailey couldn't do it.

Even as he willed his eyes to stay closed, they betrayed him.

As if they had a mind of their own, his lids flew open. His eyes rolled wildly inside his head as he madly looked around. For a few seconds he couldn't focus. All he could take in was the blackness, hanging thick and claustrophobic like a heavy veil.

It was as his vision began to clear, to pull shapes from the shadows, he suddenly felt the urge to scream, knew he could scream.

Not with terror. With happiness.

The joy flooded his body, chasing out the fear as if a fresh breeze had blown through.

There was nothing there.

No monster leaning over him, its jaws only a tooth's length from his face. No creature from hell waiting to drag him away. He must have imagined it all.

Caleb and his stupid monster rules had gotten inside his imagination and warped his mind. Just wait 'til I see Caleb at school tomorrow. He'd pay him back somehow. Maybe make up some rules of his own—robot rules, or witches rules. He'd show him how it felt to be tricked.

Breathe. In and out.

Finally, he could breathe. He pulled in a long, grateful breath of beautiful, fresh oxygen, exhaling it in a long, loud whoosh of relief.

That moment. There, as he breathed. That was his mistake, the mistake, which couldn't be undone. The rule he'd recklessly broken.

If only he'd waited. If only he'd checked.

It dawned on him, too late, there was something there, a weight, on the end of his bed.

His heart exploded.

He wasn't alone.

The thing was much smaller than he'd imagined. The size of a large dog, but uglier, blacker, and shinier. If evil could drip from a living thing, then this was dripping buckets. Its vicious teeth glowed in the dark, long and white. Its mouth pulled back as if it was smiling at him—not in a friendly way. In a hungry way.

Caleb had been right, too: the eyes did glow red, and they flashed as the thing blinked. Slowly the monster twisted its head from side to side, calmly, as if it knew Bailey wouldn't scream, couldn't scream.

Then it pulled back on its dark, scaly legs, which shimmered green even in the dark. It was preparing to launch at him. Bailey's terrified brain grasped it was coming, and instinctively he curled into a ball and covered his face with his arms.

Too bad about exposing his arms. The rules hadn't worked anyway.

He felt the air move as it leaped at him and then land on his body, its legs on either side of his hips, its black, spindly arms on top of his chest. Bailey squirmed as the claws—so sharp they felt like jagged pieces of broken glass—pierced his skin and pinned him to the bed by his shoulders.

It hurt. It really hurt. His mind screamed for his mother. His father. He'd even settle for his brother. Instead, the reply was a whistling, whispering voice, like a snake hissing senseless sounds. Then slowly the whispering built, like a swirling, whipping wind, until hundreds of voices were inside his head, talking and shrieking all at once until his own thoughts were drowned out.

A single voice arose above the sounds, louder and even more frightening. It was a wild and terrifying thing, like the wind shrieking on a stormy night. The sound began to sound familiar. It wasn't the thing, whose claws were digging into his tiny body. He suddenly understood what it was. The voice was his own, crying and begging and screaming.

He didn't want to look at the monster. It drew him as though his will was taken and stripped from him. Stopping himself from looking at it was impossible; he had to see. He looked up, and his eyes locked upon two red, ravenous orbs focused only on him. The screaming stopped for a blessed moment, and a stream of words fell from his mouth.

"I followed ... followed the rules. Followed the monster rules. It's not, not ... fair."

The thing, the monster, the stinking, dripping, red-flashing-eye creature, paused. It actually loosened its grip. Bailey thought maybe he was saved. Maybe it was letting him go.

Then it threw back its head and opened its lipless mouth. Wider and wider its dark maw opened, until the creature's face split in two and Bailey found himself staring into a black chasm. Each edge of the chasm held three rows of teeth, uneven and cracked, and as jagged as his mom's bread knife. The purpose of those teeth was very clear.

Then the voices in his head thinned to a single sound, so sharp it felt as if his head would crack open like an egg. The sound repeated like a broken recording; it took a few seconds, before he recognized it.

Laughter. Crazy, mocking laughter.

Then a sharp talon effortlessly pierced the soft flesh of his neck and tore downward in a perfect straight line. He felt his skin peel apart like a cut orange, warm blood spurting from the wound to splatter and cover his face and chest. The bitter, salty taste invaded his mouth, choking him.

Just before his eyes closed to a real death—no need to pretend anymore—the monster leaned into his face, turning its small head to the side. Its claws pinched his cheeks, and the hot scales of its skin pulled at his hair. A tongue, pointed and sticky, flicked along the outside of his ear, and its whispering, hissing voice wormed its way into his head. Laughter erupted around him and within him until his soul vibrated with it.

Then the laughter stopped and the monster paused all movement. It seemed to smile. Then it hissed through lips spreading wider and wider:

"Sometimes we change the rules."

MONSTER RULES

- Never expose your arms and legs above the bedcovers.
- Never stand next to your bed.
- Never get up at night.
- If you think there is a monster in your room, pretend to be dead.
- Do not leave closet doors open.
- Do not leave windows open.
- Only wear dark pajamas.
- Never use a heat pack or hot water bottle in bed.
- Never lie on your side.
- Never turn your back on the dark when climbing stairs.
- Don't believe in monsters—or one day you might discover they exist beyond your imagination.

FROM THE IMAGINATION VAULT

You might be thinking, *Hang on a minute, this isn't like Susan May's other stories—it's kind of simple.* Well, wonderful reader, you would be correct. This is my version of a children's story. I wrote it for my kids as a fun horror story, a little like R.L. Stine's *Goosebumps*.

With that aside, I will let you in on a little secret, and you're going to think I'm crazy. When I was a kid, I actually followed all of these rules. All except for the pajama rule. That one I made up for the story.

Most kids imagine monsters lurk, waiting to pounce when the lights go out. Growing up, I truly believed monsters were all around me, watching and waiting to pounce. I think my penchant, from a very young age, for Friday night horror films, and my passion for any horror books, may have contributed a little to my fears.*Well, okay, maybe a lot!*

My active imagination, fed often with a diet of horror, resulted in me being unable to walk outside in the dark to take out the trash, or for any other reason, without looking over my shoulder. I'm okay now, but I think I was in my late twenties before I conquered that fear.

A couple of years ago, when my boys were aged around eight and ten, I told them about all the silly rules I made up as a kid as protection from the monsters. As I told them, it dawned on me, maybe, I had a story there. In fact, I thought I could write it for my youngest son, Bailey. So I used his and his best friend's names for the characters.

I'm now well and truly grown up, and yet I still find I sleep much better when I am covered up to the neck with the bedcovers (and the heavier weight the better—much safer). I made sure the last bed we bought had a double mattress (no room for monsters under there now).

Is it any wonder when I began writing I didn't stray far from the horror and science-fiction genres? I've been sleeping surrounded by monsters for years. Don't you worry about me, though. They'll never get me, because I really do know all the monster rules ... even the ones I haven't told you.

WHERE WE ONCE WERE

Tamara dreamed of visiting her distant ancestors' 1897 time world for her PhD research paper. What she discovers is a secret two hundred years in the making. History might be about to take a different path.

WHERE WE ONCE WERE

*T*he dust surprised Tamara. The smoky-tasting powder coated her tongue and the grit stuck to her teeth. A horrible taste filtered down her throat, until she felt like gagging.

Despite her research, she'd chosen to believe her research was flawed, and she'd find green, rolling hills, neat pastures, and a quiet landscape of simple life dotted with sweet little farmhouses, with owners tending their precious land. This would prove to be the least of her dashed hopes.

Tamara surveyed the dust-blown dirt street, observing the slow meander of the town's inhabitants, as they moved between the wooden-built shops and bungalows. The buildings appeared as stark contrast to the majestic towering gum trees surrounding the settlement.

Each person nodded a friendly *hello* to the next as they passed. Three women dressed in long-sleeve, tight-fitting bodices and dark floor-sweeping skirts stopped and animatedly chatted in the middle of the street. They looked happy and comfortable, quite the opposite to how Tamara felt. She found the outfits hot and cumbersome in the stifling humidity.

How did they stand it? Tamara thought she'd melt away if forced to wear this costume for more than the few hours at a time, when she came out to mingle among the town's inhabitants.

Two children skipped along the road kicking a ball to each other. Laughing, they ducked into the shade of Werner's general store. They seemed happy, too, despite the limited luxury she'd seen so far. The flies were intolerable, too. The townsfolk and the street seemed an alien landscape, just as odd as if Tamara had been transported to Mars. Their courtesy and manners were vastly different to the brusque and impatient exchanges she often experienced in her city's bustling lifestyle.

Before her departure, she'd practiced these people's accent and mannerisms. Even though she'd grown up only one hundred odd miles away, over the centuries language had evolved so much. Common words had changed. Maybe not for the better. There was something melodic in the lack of acronyms in this time.

These people's courtesy and care was built through a common bond and had evolved from necessity. They'd only each other to rely upon. In the mid-eighteen hundreds, the first generation of arrivals to this distant, mysterious land came eager and filled with pride, refugees from a struggling life in Eastern Prussia. Lured to Australia by the Government's promise of land, they arrived hopeful and excited. The rich life imagined by the immigrants was a crafted illusion.

Quälsland (land of torment) they'd christened this place. An unwelcoming land of harsh weather, torrential rain, floods, and life-sucking droughts. Most wondered if they'd landed straight in hell.

Tamara's passion for history made her perfectly suited to study *life genetics.*Her major: 1800s through to early 1900s, colonial Australia. This was her last year of her PhD, and this trip would contribute to her final assessment. If she scored well enough, she would begin her career at Life Genetics Inc.

The obsession with *this* era and *this* town, Gatton, had begun in Tamara's childhood. In her dreams, she imagined their lives. She'd read every article published since 1850 she could find on the area. She felt as much a part of these distant relatives' lives as their DNA was of her.

When the Central University of Historical Studies advertised a scholarship for volunteers for their travel program, she surrendered an entire summer writing her submission. At twenty-four, she had preparation and, importantly, youth on her side. Being young, a consideration, as the transfer stress on the body could make things difficult. On a cellular level, the body couldn't cope with the destabilizing effect of disintegration and reform much past thirty-five. She'd heard disconcerting stories of the impact on older bodies.

After making the short list and clearing the health checks, it came down to two candidates. Tamara and Henry Cable. Both would make the trip, but the most qualified would choose the destination. The runner-up would accompany the other as an assistant. Henry's choice was 1741, Limerick, Ireland.

Henry didn't win. So here both stood under the shady veranda of a small, gray milliner's store looking out at small town life Australia, 1898.

Tamara wiped the back of her hand across her damp forehead. Rolling her dry lips between her teeth, she realized her thirst was growing by the minute. She rested a weary arm on Henry's shoulder.

The dress of the era Henry certainly suited Henry. A wide-brimmed, brown, floppy hat perched over shoulder-length hair he'd pushed casually behind his ears. A long sleeve, loose-fitting, cream shirt, open at the neck—lucky him—matched with brown brogues and suspenders, completed the look. Although Tamara would never admit it, he looked pretty cute.

"We're here. Can you believe it?"

Henry had a propensity, she'd discovered, to brood. Well, she imagined it was brooding. He didn't talk much, which simply made her talk more. Empty silences made her uncomfortable.

He took a long time to answer, continuing to stare toward the end of the street where rows of trees and dense shrubs marked the edge of town.

"I'll believe it better with a cold drink. Drowning in this humidity. God-forsaken place. Australia, ha."

The derision in his voice was thick. This wasn't his dream. Tamara knew that. She just hoped he'd remain professional. Henry had a reputation of being condescending to those he thought were less intelligent than him—which, supposedly, was everyone. Discovering he'd been beaten out of the mission leadership must have come as rather a surprise. He'd already made a few sarcastic comments, while they weren't overt, certainly hinted at sour grapes.

Tamara pulled a map from her satchel and opened it. After glancing up and down the street and returning to the map several times, she pointed toward a small wooden building across the street.

"That's the post office."

She swung her still-pointing finger farther down the road and added, "So, the hotel is that way. That's where we go. We need to get a room and start making plans."

They set off down the street. Tamara's heavy gray skirt and long-sleeved blouse itched as though the material was interwoven with barbs. Her gait felt off, due to the heaviness of the skirt and tight black boots that made her feet ache.

Would her walk give her away, make her stand out?

She'd learned the accent to perfection, but it'd never occurred to her to practice their style of movement. Suddenly, she felt uncomfortably conspicuous merely by her gait. Again, she envied Henry and his comfortable garb. He swaggered down the street as though he was born-and-bred of 1898 and not a South Pasadenan from 2123.

Despite feeling out of place and time, now Tamara was here something extraordinary had begun to happen. The town had already begun to seep beneath her skin. Once in her hotel room, she would spend the next few hours practicing her walk, her accent, and her manners, everything, so there would be no doubt she belonged.

11.13 pm, 27th December, 1898

It would happen tonight.

Three siblings, Norah, twenty-seven, Ellen, eighteen, and their brother, Michael Murphy, twenty-nine, would not see the morning.

Tamara's Gatton ancestors had been friends with the Murphy's. Letters and news-clippings chronicling the murders came to her via an unassuming time capsule. Several tatty, old shoeboxes courtesy of her great-grandmother Susanna. Thoughtfully, Susanna bundled them with other fascinating memorabilia as though she knew one day one of her descendants would need them.

Tied with red ribbon, the letters were nestled inside one box, along with a small note in flowing handwriting:

Where we once were, we must never return.

This note, though, was not from her great-great grandmother. There were other letters from Susanna inside, and when she compared the handwriting, the scrawl of this note was not that of Susanna's angular, neat style. Tamara pondered the words often, attempting to fathom exactly what they meant and for whom they were intended. Perhaps they weren't even a message about the murders. Perhaps it was the traveling music-sheet salesman Percy, mentioned so fondly in the letters?

He'd captured Susanna's heart if the long commentary passages on his hair, clothes, and the way he smiled were anything to go by. Something had happened, though, by February of 1898. After that date, mentions of him stopped abruptly. Tamara's first thought was he'd died. On checking the death notices, though, she'd discovered he'd lived until 1923.

Another mystery she hoped to solve while here.

From the letters and news articles, Tamara knew the day of the murders but not the exact time. After research, she calculated they'd occurred between ten and one am.

The murderer would strike as the Murphy's walked from a town Christmas party back to their farm homestead eight miles from town. For some reason no one could explain, they left the open road to take an unnecessary detour along a dark path through the bush.

A half-mile down the path, their bodies would be found the afternoon of the next day after an extensive search by most of the townsfolk. Ellen and Norah's arms were bound with their own silk dress belts, their heads bashed until unrecognizable. They had been propped up, sitting against a towering gum tree as though merely resting in the shade.

Since forensics and crime scene investigation at the time were rudimentary, the medical examiner had not recorded if either girl was raped. Tamara supposed that could have been one motive, although it didn't really explain the ferocity of the attack.

Their brother must have tried to protect them, and met his death before preventing the inevitable. Michael's body would be found, beaten and mutilated, with a final gunshot wound to the temple.

The strangest part was a note made at the bottom of one of the report's pages. Inside each girl's mouth was found a key. Tamara could find no mention of whether the key belonged to the girls or the killer. Keys weren't a regular item of the period, locks only being perfected in the 1800s and not widely used. Most people didn't have enough valuables to warrant protection. The Murphy family was not rich, so it was doubtful the keys belonged to them.

So *there* was another mystery. Whose keys were they? Why insert them in the dead girls' mouths?

Her heart fluttered at the thought of being here, just over two hundred years later, poised to discover the truth of the worst unsolved crime in the colony's early history.

Squatting behind a bush by the roadside, Tamara shifted in the uncomfortable position trying to ease the ache, which had begun to claw at her calves. She looked over at Henry, a few feet away. He leaned against a stocky tree, slowly chewing on a piece of grass—he really had adapted to his role—his face half in shadow.

His stance was as nonchalant as his attitude had been most of the afternoon. Tamara had barely controlled her annoyance. It didn't help at all the clothes and styling of the era really suited him. Something about long, unkempt hair on a man wearing a slouch hat and a careless attitude was rather attractive. The *Mr. Darcy* affect she'd coined it.

Henry wasn't even bothering to maintain a pretense of interest. His back was to the road as he stared across the darkened, peaceful, land behind them. In their time, this kind of untouched natural vista only existed in certain carefully maintained and protected reserves. These reserves, so popular as holiday and weekend destinations, were booked out months ahead. In peak summer season, it came down to a lottery, even for a day visit.

A flare of anger rose in Tamara as she considered had the roles been reversed, she would have remained professional. Words rose in her throat, but she swallowed them down. Instead, keeping her voice calm, she said, "Henry, you do have the camera equipment calibrated correctly, right? One chance is all we have to get this."

Henry's head turned to her. He stared at her for long seconds as though she'd spoken a foreign language, which required time for translation.

"I'm standing here, aren't I?"

"That means what?"

"It's done."

He leaned to the side and spat the chewed grass onto the ground, then sent her a piercing don't-ask-me-again stare, before resuming his observation of the land.

The camera to which she referred, was fixed in a tree branch above the spot the Murphy's would meet their death. Set to follow voice and movement, the equipment should capture everything. The only issue being, the sensitivity of the sensors.

If the event happened outside its range, they would have nothing.

Tamara had surmised the murders occurred beneath the tree, because that's where the women's bodies were found. If the killer had done the deed elsewhere, all they would capture would be him placing the bodies beneath the tree.

Maybe a good thing thought Tamara, not overly keen on watching three innocent people murdered. At the least, they would get a look at the murderer.

During the afternoon, while waiting in the hotel room, they'd made a plan to hide themselves near the point where the Murphy's would leave the road. At the very least, they could witness why the three had left the road.

As Tamara watched Henry chewing on yet another piece of grass that waved in the air in time with his mouth movement, she decided to broach the subject of his attitude. Get it out of the way, so they could focus on their work.

"Henry, we need to talk. I—"

The sound of voices stopped her. Instantly, she turned back to the road and leaned forward, crouching lower behind the bush. Henry ducked down and moved to join her. She noted his nimbleness. He was as lithe as a cat, when he wanted to be.

The murmur of female voices down the road. A giggle. Then, the deeper tone of a man.

Every second, they grew closer.

Tamara's heart galloped, the pounding suddenly so loud she imagined if the group passed too close to her, they'd hear her. The Murphys would leave the road to their final destiny across the way from them, so she knew it had to be them.

As they came into view around the corner, Tamara suddenly realized some of what she knew about this night was wrong.

There were the Murphy's, yes, laughing, talking, and weaving along the road without a care in the world, never knowing shortly they'd laugh no more.

They weren't alone.

Alongside them walked two others. A man and a woman. These

two seemed as much a part of the group as the siblings. Clearly, they were comfortable in each other's company.

Norah and Ellen walked arm-in-arm. On the other side of Ellen the other woman kept pace with them, her arm, also, linked with Ellen's. The *stranger*—as Tamara thought of the man—strolled casually beside Thomas, animatedly talking. His was the voice Tamara had heard. Thomas seemed to be attentively listening and nodding.

Suddenly, the stranger stopped as though he'd seen something unexpected. Tamara lowered herself further down behind the bush. She could still see a little through the foliage if she bent a small branch to the side. The man pointed to the slip rail fence across from Tamara and Henry's hiding spot. This was where the path began. He leaned in and whispered something to Michael, but Tamara couldn't hear with the girl's giggling and gossiping about people at the dance, they'd just left.

She cursed the fact she had only one camera and it was at the murder site. If she'd been able, she would have brought a second. Then she could have had it here to pick up these unknown unfolding events. However, bringing technology through was kept to a minimum. *A*, it could be discovered, and that wouldn't be an easy discussion. *B*, the transfer of inanimate objects required greater energy and posed unnecessary risk.

The group was almost alongside their hiding position. From the corner of her eye, Tamara noticed Henry raising his head slightly to get a better look.

Now he was interested.

His problem, she realized was he was a *S.A.P.* Short attention span. Typical of his personality type. *A Mr. Darcy SAP, in fact.*

The group was so close Tamara detected the faint scent of sweat mingled with a not unpleasant musk scent. *Perfume maybe?* The stranger and Michael clambered over the fence. Michael almost cleared it with a single bound. To her surprise, the three women, in a very unladylike move, hitched their skirts and clambered over the fence.

Thomas and the stranger held out hands to help them over. Two made it over easily, but Ellen slipped as she mounted the post and almost fell. The stranger saved her, catching her in his arms, before lifting her the rest of the way. This elicited another round of giggles from the three girls.

Without waiting, they set off down the path, casual as can be, quickly disappearing into the bush. The stranger didn't immediately follow, lingering, slowly turning back, until he faced in Tamara's direction. He stared back up the road for a moment, as though he were looking for something. Or someone.

Was he checking if they'd been seen? Waiting for an accomplice? Perhaps he was just checking to ensure nothing had been dropped as they'd clambered over the fence. Or had he felt they were being watched?

The full moon snuck out from behind a cloud, lighting the surrounds in a white-gold glow. The trees alongside the road took on a human quality as though they were silent witnesses to events that would echo through time.

All the planets—and moon—are aligning, thought Tamara.

The moonlight illuminated the stranger clearly, revealing his facial details as though he were spot lit on a stage.

Tamara couldn't help herself. She gasped, but immediately shoved the knuckles of both hands into her mouth to stifle the sound.

She *knew* the face.

It was impossible. Yet, as she thought it through, it *was* probable. There'd been no record of *him* being with the Murphys that night. That's what had surprised her.

She was certain, though, his identity unmistakable. She'd studied his photographs for years, staring at them, adding details on her ePad App to animate him, create an A.I. animation with whom she could converse. She saw now the voice she'd given him was not quite right. This man's voice was lower with a richer timbre. He could be a singer it was so melodic. His hawk nose, sharp jaw, and that flop of dark hair, so very familiar it took her long moments to assure herself she wasn't imagining any of this.

Two hundred years before she was born, here was the face of the man who'd tucked her into bed throughout her childhood. Who'd nicknamed her Tamacious—a marriage of her name and tenacious. A man she hadn't seen in five years since his death, which she still struggled to believe.

One difference separated her memory of her father and this man. The eyes. The stranger's eyes held an emptiness she'd never seen in her father's. Even the last time she'd seen him, when he looked so defeated. There was no doubt in her mind, though; she was looking at her great-great-grandfather.

Then he was gone, following the woman, and the Murphys on their way to meet Fate.

Tamara racked her brain. She couldn't remember what the articles had said about her great-great grandfather's whereabouts on the night. If, he was even mentioned. She couldn't recall. When she got back to her time, she would need to conduct more research. What was he doing there? Surely, *surely,* it wasn't him, who—. If it was, did she really want to discover if her ancestor was a brutal murderer? He couldn't be. No, she didn't believe that. Something must have happened.

Tamara turned to Henry beside her. His gaze continued to stare where the stranger, no, her great-great-grandfather had just stood. Slowly, he turned to look at her.

"That's unexpected," he said.

Henry obviously hadn't noticed the resemblance to her or, if he did, was pretending otherwise.

"I've suddenly lost my taste for history," Tamara said, more to herself than to him.

Henry gave her one of his *you're-a-crazy-woman* looks she hated with a passion.

"Too late girl. History just took its path."

A thought suddenly occurred to Tamara.

Why did history and fate have to take this path? They were here *right now*, and the thought her ancestor might be involved or maybe be killed or kidnapped suddenly felt terrifying. What if he hadn't yet married, if her great-great-grandmother hadn't given birth yet to their only child? What if somehow Tamara and Henry's visit had changed everything? She couldn't imagine what they'd done. There'd been no mention of the Murphy's leaving the town with anyone. So this could be a time line kink.

Oh, God, what should she do?

Tamara stood rather clumsily. Her muscles felt weak after crouching for so long, and she swayed drunkenly until she recovered her balance. Then she was off, running toward the slip rail on the opposite side of the road. She could hear Henry chasing behind her.

"Wait, what are you doing? Where are you going, Tamara? Tamara?"

Tamara didn't stop. She didn't turn around or answer. One blistering idea consumed her: Tonight, history might be about to take a different path. She couldn't let that happen.

FROM THE IMAGINATION VAULT

I wrote *Where We Once Were* in 2012. I'd had this idea in my head around the old time slip trope: If you went back in time and killed one of your grandparents would you simply blink out of existence? The theory goes, you would never be born if your grandparent wasn't around to give life to one of your parents. Nobody ever addresses the meme, though, why would you kill your own grandparent? I pondered if you were to risk your very existence by killing a grandparent, maybe there would be a very good reason to do so.

My mother's ancestors emigrated to Gatton, Queensland Australia from Prussia in the late 1800s. While researching my family tree for another story I read articles about the terribly difficult and disappointing life they encountered upon arrival. Growing up in Brisbane (about two hours drive away), we occasionally drove past Gatton. Many a time a discussion would ensue about the mysterious, unsolved Gatton murders. I always wondered about the details and would quiz my parents, but they only knew the basics. After all, it had occurred more than seventy plus years before. Even so, the legend lived on and talk of it was as though it had happened only recently.

What a fascinating story it would make to explore the concept of meeting your ancestors with the backdrop and mystery of the unsolved murders. Plus it would give me an excuse to research and imagine my distant relatives' lives. Writing sometimes feels very much like time travel. You truly feel as though you're there. I wanted a trip to a *real* past that was personal.

The story lay filed away, unnoticed, on my laptop for three years. I didn't give it a second thought until I decided to dust it off for this collection. To my surprise, as I went through what I thought would be a quick edit, I became engrossed in the story and the characters. The original 1,700 word short became 3,100 odd words. If I wasn't in the middle of edits for my next book *The Troubles Keeper (released October 2016)* and prepped to go on the book after that *Best Seller (released 2018)*, I think I would have started writing the novel immediately.

My mind now spins occasionally with the possibilities and questions about the characters and the mysteries raised in this short passage. The *Henry* character, who initially had about three lines in the original story, decided he would become very involved. He even demanded to be referenced as Mr. Darcy from one of my favorite stories and films Jane Austen's *Pride and Prejudice*.

Now, I'm not saying *absolutely*, but don't be surprised if *Where We Once Were* turns up as a novel in the future. Something tells me Tamara, Henry and the fictional world I've begun to build in Gatton and back in our traveler's home time won't be satisfied with a short story. *Where We Once Were* might actually be for me, where I'm going in the very near future. Ain't imagination a wonderful thing?

If you would like to read the novel of this short story, do drop me a line at susanmay@node1.com.au. Just for writing to me I will include you in my early readers' mailing list for a free e-copy when I write it.

So don't be shy. I always reply to my emails. After all, you are the person I am writing for and where you would like to travel next is important to me.

Update

The novel of Where We Once Were is a go! So many readers have written begging for the novel how can I not write it? So I traveled to Gatton in 2016 for research to ensure I get the feel right and I will begin writing the story in 2020 with a publication date sometime that year. If you would like to receive an update of the progress and possibly a free or discounted early copy of the novel please write to me at susanmay@node1.com.au.

Come join my private Facebook group **Susan Mayhem Gang,** as I now have several videos filmed from my trip to Gatton posted there.

DESPERATE

Two agitated women inexplicably run out into oncoming freeway traffic. One is run over by a lorry; the other flung in the air by a car. They should be dead. Not only do they survive, despite horrific injuries and police intervention, they seem determined to continue to the other side of the roadway. Are they insane or is their desperation due to stakes so high they're prepared to give their lives?

DESPERATE

It happened so suddenly Peter Millpole didn't have time to react. One minute he was happily driving in the outside lane of the highway listening to some mindless tune that seemed to have more talk than melody. Next, it was as though an enormous tree trunk was dropped from the sky onto his Volkswagen Polo.

Just before the impact he'd noticed a yellow flash streak from the shoulder. He'd had only a moment to curse litterbugs for leaving trash to blow onto the freeway before there was a huge bang, followed by the implosion of his windshield and a sound he never wanted to hear again. A shredding, popping explosion filled his entire world as a thousand cracks and fractures blinded his view.

The shock caused his leg muscles to twitch and his foot to slip from the accelerator. This movement and the force of the collision slowed the car sufficiently so that he'd almost stopped before realizing he needed to use the brake. Every extremity of his body tingled with the fire of adrenaline.

His grip on the steering wheel felt super-human. Sitting there seeing nothing, hearing nothing and only knowing something

terrible had happened, he took a moment to call on his police officer's experience (even though he'd been retired for four years now).
Inhaling and exhaling three deep calming breaths he slowed his
racing heart.

What the hell had he hit? And how?

Shoving open the door Peter heard multiple voices from all
directions.

A man's voice: "Stop."

A woman's voice: "What the hell?"

Another man's voice: "Oh my God! What?"

As he stepped out of his car a god-awful sound of screeching
brakes caused him to brace. Though if he were hit bracing probably
wouldn't save him.

The next second he saw an articulated-lorry in the next lane slam
into something—another horrific, sickening thud—and come to a
screaming halt twenty feet or so ahead.

What the hell was happening? Was it war? Terrorists?

A policeman bolted past the front of his car toward the lorry.

Another ran by him in the opposite direction waving his hands.
As he passed he called, "You right buddy?"

Peter nodded but he didn't think the man saw because his full
attention was now focused on stopping the traffic behind.

Making his way around his car Peter wondered how the police
had arrived so quickly. Less than a minute had elapsed and he now
counted four officers.

He saw now that two people had been hit.

Several yards along the road a policewoman crouched over the
prostrate body of a young woman; her long, straight hair, strewn in a
blonde tangle, covered her face. An arm bent at a grotesque angle,
was only one of her serious injuries. If she didn't have some kind of
spinal injury she'd be lucky.

Her body lay deathly still twisted in an unnatural way as though
she possessed a hinged stomach, while a policewoman—obviously
the owner of the *what-the-hell* voice—tended to her.

Peter made his way to the pair to crouch next to them.

Suddenly the woman became conscious, moaning and beginning to cry. Seconds later droplets of bloodied spit erupted from her mouth as she attempted to speak.

"Leeese," she said.

Please Peter figured she was saying.

Blood trickled down the side of her face from a split on her temple. Already the injury had raised to a nasty, white lump that might mean cranial bleeding.

Glancing back at his crumpled hood and imploded windshield Peter wondered how she'd even survived.

Without diverting her attention from the moaning woman the policewoman spoke to him.

"You the driver?"

"Yes. But I ... she ran out in front of me. There was no time."

"I know. We saw everything."

Peter released a breath, and he realized he'd been holding his breath.

"In fact this one and the other one—we think they're twins—have been playing dodgems with the traffic. We'd stopped them. Then this crazy bitch ..." She nodded at the groaning woman, "took off."

I stared down at the woman. Her mouth moved but the words were so low to be inaudible.

The policewoman continued as though she needed to get the events off her chest.

"Mike grabbed her but her jacket came off in his hands. Thank Christ it did or you may have hit him too. When you hit her the other one made a break and ..." She angled her head toward the stopped truck in the next lane "the truck got her."

In his thirty-three years on the force Peter had never heard of such a thing. Neither had this officer by the wild look in her eyes.

"Is the other one okay?"

"Dunno. One of us is with her."

She shook her head. "Insanity."

The blonde stirred, suddenly more alive and coherent like she'd received an electric shock. Her accent was strange. Guttural. To Peter it sounded harsh, almost Germanic. Maybe Swedish? Something Nordic at least.

"Leease. Help me. I need to be up. *Please.* Must go."

Placing her palm on the blonde's head and gently stroking her hair, the officer soothed, "Ma'am, you're not going anywhere. You're badly injured. Help is on the way."

Around them passengers and drivers from other stopped cars— the lucky ones, who wouldn't have to live with the memory of a shattering windshield, the terrifying sound and the resultant horror of colliding with a human being—began to gather. The crowd stood mesmerized, gaping and whispering as though this were a television soap opera. Wondering at human voyeurism, Peter felt grateful and satisfied to see another officer herd them to the shoulder.

Good thinking. Who knew what would happen if following traffic didn't stop in time. It would only take one going too fast.

Peter and the policewoman's attention was momentarily diverted by the crowd and so they were unprepared for the woman to suddenly sit up and instantly climb to her feet. Before they could react she'd gained a few yards of separation. She glanced back at them and then continued at a trot toward the center of the highway.

Was she actually heading for the other side? Was she going to run out into more traffic? What the?

Echoing his own thoughts, the officer muttered, "What the?" and "How in hell?"

Exactly! How? Peter thought.

At least one of her arms was shattered and her hip looked dislocated.

In fact double, triple how?

Instinct pushed Peter to his feet and he was chasing her when, at his age, he had no business running anywhere anymore, let alone after some freak of a woman. So many years on the force just embedded quick, unthinking reaction into your being. *Move quickly or die quickly.*

She was already over the highway barrier and running along the busy lanes filled with speeding traffic traveling in the opposite direction.

Suicidal, that's all he could think.

"Stop," Peter shouted as cars slowed and drove around her.

Ahead of Peter another officer came from the other side of the road along the shoulder. If Peter continued from the inside and the officer from there, they could trap her in the middle. The officer clearly having the same thought twirled a hand in the air to signal the maneuver to Peter.

The blonde's head whiplashed back and forth between Peter, the officer and the vacant forested area beyond the highway.

With them closing in on her she seemed to panic, freeze and become uncertain of her next move. Peter and the officer accelerated, and suddenly they had her.

"No, no, no!" she screamed, her attention now fully on Peter as he reached for her. She waved her arms in the air as though trying to create a distraction. This gave the officer a chance to come from behind and he clamped a firm hand on her arm.

When she whirled to look at her captor Peter seized her other arm. Her reaction was as though they'd unleashed a demon. She kicked and twisted violently, with the strength of a two hundred pound wrestler and not a young, petite woman.

How could she fight with at least one broken limb?

She flailed so crazily Peter felt his grip loosening, and the thought crossed his mind that she might have the strength to even break his wrist.

He still hadn't recovered from his chase of her and his breath came in short, sharp gasps as he struggled to keep hold. He wanted to let go but if he did she could be killed. Even worse she might kill some poor driver or hapless passenger.

"Nooo, fuck you!" she screamed and spat at them both. "Let go. Police! Police!"

"We're police. Stop. Stop it. Calm. Down," the officer said, he too sounding out of breath.

Suddenly two more men-in-blue and another man appeared. Between the five of them they managed to lift her spread-eagled from the ground.

Now she kicked and bucked as though they carried her to her death. Even with five strong men, they struggled to keep a grasp on her as they maneuvered her from the road.

"Police. Help! I need police."

"We're the police. *Calm down*," one of the new officers said.

"No! I don't believe yooou."

The men wrestled the thrashing woman to the ground. The civilian—young, jeans and trendy t-shirt—braced his forearm to her chest while the others pinned her legs and arms.

"Fuck man," said the civilian. "She's got incredible strength. Some crazy drug trip for sure."

Peter stood back as two police zip-tied her legs and then her arms.

The protruding bone in her arm waved as she fought her bindings. Despite her serious injuries it had taken five of them to get her under control.

Freakish sprung to mind as Peter watched the police trying to calm her, to no avail. His breath came in ragged, halting mouthfuls as he tried to assess what had actually happened.

Then he saw the other girl.

Lying deathly still behind the truck's back wheels was an identical blonde. Just like her sister, her hair fanned out around her as though she were lying on a beach and not in the middle of a black asphalt roadway.

This twin wasn't putting up a fight. Attending to her was the policewoman he'd first met.

A squawking, male voice erupted from her two-way. "What's happening? Over."

"Second woman seriously injured. Still breathing."

As Peter approached the two he noticed a man sitting on the side of the road. By his expressionless face and the way he kept looking at the girl and then staring up at the sky he figured it was the unfortunate lorry driver. Clearly the poor schmuck was in shock.

What surprised Peter as he drew closer was that this twin was actually conscious and talking. In a repeat performance, like her sister had done, she suddenly sprung to life and attempted to get up. Her body from the waist upward contorted like a flapping fish out of water.

"Stay still. You *must* stay still. You're badly hurt. Ma'am do you hear me? You cannot get up."

The policewoman spoke firmly, though her voice kept cracking. *Stress, probably.*

By the look of this girl's twisted body she didn't have much choice when it came to lying there. Still, her body continued to flex in a failed attempts to rise.

"Can I help?" Peter said.

The policewoman looked up with eyes filled with so many emotions. Fear, horror, disbelief. Her mouth, a thin line of anxiety, barely moved as she spoke.

"Can you stay with her? The ambulance is four minutes out. I need to guide it in."

Before Peter could answer she was up and running toward a gathered group of people on the edge of the stopped cars.

Squatting next to the blonde, Peter couldn't believe her injuries. A line of vivid red trickled from her mouth. One arm, black and swollen, moved back and forth up and down her body as though she were searching for something. Her legs must have been run over by the lorry. They were shattered to a pulp, as though they'd exploded. Blood splattered on the road about them as though a giant's hand had swatted her like she was a mosquito. A patch of hair was gone, ripped from the side of her head along with part of her scalp. Blood was everywhere.

Gruesome. That was the word.

Peter reached for her hand, trying to stop its violent movement. God knows how much damage had been done to her back. She needed to be still to minimize further injury. That's if she survived.

The second he crouched beside her she addressed him, even though she was facing away. She couldn't turn her head toward him but she started talking anyway. Her speech was surprisingly clear, but desperation enclosed her words. Immediately Peter stood and moved around her body to look in her eyes. He wanted her to see the concern in his face, understand someone was there who cared.

"Help me. I must go."

Déjà Vu. Same words as her twin.

"Go where?"

"Please. They're waiting."

The strange halting accent again. It wasn't German. No. He was pretty certain now it was Swedish. Years ago he'd had a thing for the redhead Frida from Abba and had watched several documentaries on the group. This was the same accent.

"Calm down" was all he could think to say as he rested his hand on her cheek. The skin felt unusually cold. A vein on her right temple pulsed rhythmically. He wondered if that was normal or a result of the accident. Noticing a pool of blood, growing beneath the torn side of her head, Peter prayed the ambulance arrived soon or they would have made a pointless journey.

The blonde suddenly jerked her neck up off the ground, interrupting his thoughts. She craned sideways to look past him.

Again, how the hell was she moving like that?

"Must get to other side. They wait for me."

She lowered her head back to the ground and looked into his eyes.

In the moment their eyes met a peculiar feeling shivered through Peter's body. Something wasn't right with her. Well, that was an understatement, but besides the extraordinary behavior, physically, she ... she looked not human.

A strange golden color surrounded her irises, the color so bright it seemed to glow despite the full sunlight. He'd never seen eyes like these. Her tongue, too, it seemed too deep a red like she'd sucked on a raspberry-flavored water ice.

Could it be shock? Loss of blood?

Before he had time to speak, she added, "On the other side. They wait."

"Who's there? Who's waiting?"

She was out of her mind. The impact. Her injuries. Had to be.

"Others. My people."

She made another pitiful effort to raise her body. The action reminded Peter of an injured, downed animal making a futile attempt to rise and escape a predator just before the fatal bite. Considering the damage her strength and determination were incredible.

Applying gentle pressure to her shoulders Peter pushed her back down.

"You will help me?"

She stared hopefully at him, her strange golden eyes flashing.

"Get ... to my people. Please. Otherwise ... we die."

Despite the intenseness of her voice this one spoke more calmly than her twin.

Still, they both seemed desperate to cross the highway to the opposite shoulder.

"Who will die?"

Realizing suddenly that she must mean her twin he added, "Your sister's alive."

More than alive, crazy alive, superhuman alive he thought to add.

Instead he said, "Don't worry. You're the one we need to help."

"Not my sister."

"Well, you sure look alike."

"Clone you call us. Specially selected. Me. One of us must return. We came for impregnation. Must return. Fertilized. Genetic failure continues with each, with each generation. Two more cycles and we all die."

Delirious was Peter's immediate thought.

In an attempt to keep her calm and conscious he asked, "Cycle?"

"Our world moves within two light years of yours every eight hundred and forty years. Close enough for portal. Last chance this time. One of us must get to the portal before it closes."

"How long before it closes?" Peter asked, thinking he'd dine out for years on this story.

"Fifteen twenty-one. And thirty-two seconds. Please. Now. Help. We are near. Other side of vehicle-way. Please. You will take me?"

Peter stared at his watch. Strangely when he stared at the time-piece the second hand seemed to tick more slowly as though at the mere mention of an interstellar portal time had suddenly changed.

He looked across the road to where she kept glancing. The traffic had come to a standstill. People were out of their cars milling around, confused.

He looked back at the girl; her eyes found his. He was struck by a strange glow, which seemed to emanate from every pore of her skin. As he stared the glow seemed to intensify.

Drugs? Must be drugs.

He'd seen something like this with angel dust. Not quite this but God knows what they put in the shit these days. This one and her sister, the other supposed clone, would awaken in hospital later with the worst hangover of their lives. That's if this one survived.

Regardless of her illusions the fact now stood that her imaginary portal would close in—he checked his watch again—nine minutes and twenty seconds. In her condition, her body so mutilated, she wasn't going anywhere, least of all across the road in that time whether he helped her or not.

When Peter looked away from his watch he saw she was now unconscious. Laying there, her eyes closed, she now looked like an ordinary but terribly injured, young woman. Nothing alien about her. He must be in shock himself for that thought to cross his mind.

Three minutes later the ambulance arrived and the medics raced over to them. Quickly they began attending to her.

No longer needed Peter stood and backed away to stand alone to the side to watch the men work on her. They checking her vitals, before placing a brace around her neck and gently moving her on to a stretcher.

Peter checked his watch again.

Three-nineteen.

Without consciously making the decision he walked across the road, moving between the still-milling people and the stationary cars. Nobody noticed him, the spectacle of the accident so all consuming. Reaching the other side he climbed the concrete barricade and then carefully slid-walked down the ten-foot grass incline beyond.

He now found himself in a small, open area surrounded by trees and shrubs. He stopped, rotating on the spot as he scanned the vista.

What the hell was he thinking? Did he really expect some kind of alien portal? *Really?*

The accident. The shock. He'd need to get a check up to see if his brain had been knocked loose, purely because he'd even considered checking here.

His first thought when he saw the golden flash was *lightning*. He caught the vision from the corner of his eye. The light seemed about fifty feet away just before a clump of trees at the edge of the glade.

He raised his hand to his brow to shield the sun, thinking the anomaly was some kind of reflection from a car mirror from the highway.

Peter took a few steps forward and stopped, blinking from the rapidly increasing glow. There was something there.

Actually *something real* there.

Not a reflection. Not the sun or a weird trick of light. Something crazy.

Two blonde women, identical to the two on the freeway, stood unmoving, looking back at him. They dressed in brilliant, white suits that clung to their bodies like a second skin. Between them hovered a shimmering, gold orb about the size of a Chinese gong.

A sudden brilliant color burst exploded outward from the sphere piercing his eyes. Peter's hands flew to his face and his palms dug into his eyes pushing at the sharp pain.

Seconds later when he opened them again he was just in time to see the blonde pair step together, hover as if frozen in space, then disappear inside the glow as if forcefully pulled.

Then the image was gone. No glow. No golden light. No women. Just trees and grass and shrubs and the sounds of emergency vehicles behind him.

Instinctively he glanced at his watch. Three twenty-two.

The portal had closed.

Peter shook his head determinedly, as though the motion would somehow remove the image from his mind.

What the hell?

He rubbed his forehead and looked around. Nobody was there. Nobody had seen what he'd seen. Slowly he turned and walked back to the road. His mind filled with just one thought *shock sure can mess with your mind.*

Desperately he hoped that was true.

FROM THE IMAGINATION VAULT

It's a while ago since I wrote this story. *Desperate* was one of the first stories I wrote in 2010 after deciding to pursue my life-long dream of a writing career. As I write this *Imagination Vault* five years later, I can still vividly remember watching the YouTube video which inspired this tale.

https://youtu.be/47ZUI1TMoaU

During the edit for inclusion in this *Behind Dark Doors* collection I re-watched the video. Intriguingly and to my horror, I learned that two days after the video, one of these women went on to murder a man who'd taken the least injured of the sisters in to his home. A 2012 documentary details the entire incident and aftermath.

https://youtu.be/9-bIWmo8eJc

WARNING: Both these videos include violence and swearing and are disturbing.

More information:

https://en.wikipedia.org/wiki/Ursula_and_Sabina_Eriksson

When I saw the initial video the only explanation that seemed logical was a mind-altering drug. As it turned out the truth was even more bizarre.

The Swedish twins Ursula and Sabina Eriksson suffered from a rare psychiatric disorder folie à deux, a shared psychosis in which Ursula's delusional beliefs were transmitted to her sister Sabina.

Sabina, the lesser injured of the two, was released from court two days after the incident. On the same day she went on to murder Glenn Hollinshead, a generous man simply trying to help her. He'd been walking his dog with a friend and came upon the woman behaving oddly. Worried for her, he offered her assistance and some-where to stay overnight. The next morning, for his trouble, she stabbed him to death with a kitchen knife.

Fascinating and horrible in equal proportions.

When I wrote *Desperate* the event had just occurred and even though I Googled for days in 2010, I found no answers. This story was my fictional explanation of why two people would behave so bizarrely. Mine is fantasy but the real life story still sounds just as fantastical. Who knows what is the truth. All I'm left with is that sometimes fact is *definitely* stranger than fiction.

BEHIND MORE DARK DOORS

I hope you enjoyed your visit behind dark doors with my short story.

You can find more short stories in my Behind Dark Doors Collections and soon to be released Destination Dark Zone.

From time to time, I'll release more volumes as I write more short stories in between my novels.

COLLECTIONS

Destination Dark Zone
(COMING MARCH 2019)

Behind Dark Doors (one)
Behind Dark Doors (two)
Behind Dark Doors (three)
Behind Dark Doors (the complete collection)
(Includes one, two and three)

STAY IN TOUCH WITH SUSAN MAY

Join Susan May's Ultimate Reader Experience and receive a Susan May starter library of free books.

www.susanmaywriter.net/free-books

You will receive free stories to keep.

plus

- *Behind the Story* access to fascinating details about the writing of Susan's books.
- Contests to enter with great prizes like Kindle readers and Audible books.
- Free and discounted book offers

- And much more (we're working on the *much more* all the time)

You can find Susan May every day at her private Facebook group **The Mayhem Gang.** You are welcome to join a great bunch of people there from around the world, discussing books, life and other fun topics.

www.facebook.com/groups/ReaderMayhem/

Connect with Susan May
www.susanmaywriter.net/free-books
susanmay@node1.com.au

DEAR READER, A FAVOR ...

If you have enjoyed this story or any of my books, can I ask you a favor please?

If you have a spare few minutes, could you please visit the online store from which you purchased **Behind Dark Doors (two)** and leave a short review (a long one if you like). Reviews help a book gain an audience.

I'd love to hear from you too, so feel free to email me susanmay@node1.com.au or find me on Facebook or Twitter. You will absolutely make this author's day.

ABOUT SUSAN MAY

Susan May sold more than 150,000 books and is an Amazon best-selling author, ranked among the top one hundred horror authors in the USA since 2015.

Her growing number of fans from all over the world have likened her immersive and page turning style to Stephen King, Dean Koontz, Robert Mathieson, Gillian Flynn and Ray Bradford.

Susan was four when she decided she would become a writer and packed a bag to march down the road looking for a school. For forty-six years after, she suffered from life-gets-in-the-way-osis. Setting a goal to write just one page a day cured her in 2010. This discipline grew into an addictive habit, which has since born multiple best-selling dark thriller novels and dozens of short stories and novellas, many of which are published award-winners in Australia, the U.S.A and the U.K.

Passionate film lover since childhood, Susan is also a film critic with the dream job of reviewing films for a local radio station. You'll find her several times a week in a darkened cinema gobbling popcorn and enjoying the latest film. She sees 150 plus films a year on screen at the invitation of all the studios and, no, she never tires of them.

Susan lives in beautiful Perth, Western Australia with her two teenage sons and husband, while her mind constantly travels to dark, faraway places most would fear to visit. That though is where her inspiration lives, so go she must.

THE TROUBLES KEEPER PREVIEW

Enjoy the opening opening chapters of Susan May's International best selling novel The Troubles Keeper.

HE SAVES OTHERS FROM THEIR TROUBLES. WHO WILL SAVE HIM?

Most of us are lucky if we have one friend to simply be there when we're down. Well, meet bus driver Rory Fine, who possesses the unique gift of relieving others of their troubles. For real! Strangers, friends, anyone he passes by, he can help. With just the barest of touches, for a while, the troubles in their hearts simply fade away.

It's his way of making the world a better place, by giving people the chance to get out from under the weight of their woes. His bus-driving job is perfect because it allows him to meet so many people every day. And all of them are completely unaware why being near him makes them feel happier and more able to face life's struggles.

There's another bonus, too. He's smitten with one of his regulars, sweet Mariana, but he can't find the courage to even say hello. He's shy and awkward and, well, different because of his gift.

Until one stormy night, when he makes a bold announcement to his passengers. Upon disembarking, he suggests they offload their worries into his palm. This might present the perfect chance for him to finally speak to the girl he thinks he just might love.

But...

There's a killer aboard, and he leaves behind something darker and more terrifying than troubles. Soon Rory will discover a powerful entity also seeks Mariana, but his intentions have nothing to do with love.

Can a gentle soul such as he, stand the remotest chance of stopping a cold, relentless evil?

. . .

To do so, he'll face more than this enemy. He'll face his own harrowing past. But he will need to find a way to overcome everything he fears. For not only is Mariana in terrible danger but the very fabric of the world is at stake.

From international best selling suspense author Susan May, comes another page-turner keeping readers awake way past their bedtime. Board The Troubles Keeper for a non-stop killer suspense ride. Meet memorable characters you'll love and a world you won't want to leave.

... and since the eBook is **FREE in KINDLE UNLIMITED or** a few dollars to own, and also available in **paperback** and **whisper-synched audible**, there's no better time to board this wonderful, killer suspense ride!

"Not since Dean Koontz's Odd Thomas have I enjoyed a character as much as I do Rory Fine!" Carolyn Werner

"Susan May seems to be following in the footsteps of **Stephen King.** I, for one, have already put her on my *'If she writes it, I will read it'* list." Madelon Wilson *(Good Reads Reviewer USA)*

"A unique take on a serial killer and the author is brilliant at creating a storyline that leaves the reader breathless." Maureen Ellis *(Good Reads reviewer UK)*

Now read the first four chapters of the book readers say they cannot put down ...

The
Troubles
Keeper

INTERNATIONAL BEST SELLING AUTHOR

SUSAN MAY

1

*H*e examines his work. Certainly not the best he's done but not the worst either. He's improving and becoming more artful. More certain and confident. There's magic in this moment; the *just after* moment when he can breathe again. *In. And out.* A drowning man reaching the surface to suck in pure air so he can survive.

Disappointment rushes in as he feels her last breath. He feels the failure like an ache inside ripping at his core. He felt so certain his search was over, but he was wrong.

He'd found her on the bus. Something had attracted him to *that* bus. Surely the girl, he'd thought. He'd sat behind her as they had traveled downtown. Pretending he'd dropped something, he'd leaned forward. In the closeness he smelled her hair like a bee smells nectar. Sweet. Enticing.

After the bus ride she'd met a friend. A girl just like her, unsuspecting and unaware. As she'd touched her friend, greeting her with a kiss, *there* was the glow, the shine of what lay beneath, inside, where only he could reach down.

At the cinema she was merely four rows away when he saw the

shine. Surrounding her, glowing in the dark, a gentle halo of gold as she leaned to her friend to whisper something. They'd laughed, before returning their attention to shared popcorn and the film.

From the multiplex he'd followed, watching from a distance from doorways and shop fronts, pretending to peer into windows. She'd shouted a goodbye to the other—her final goodbye. She hadn't known, so certain there will always be just one more. Does anyone ever recognize their last of anything?

All hope is gone as she slumps. One leg stretched before her, the other bent back beneath the chair like a mannequin awaiting display. Moments before her hands gripped the chair's arms like claws. Now they lay unfurled and limp.

Blood flows in rivulets from the thin, white line carved in her forehead. Red against shiny white bone and pale, translucent skin. Shimmer-black hair falls about her face; strands caught in the blood. He considers brushing them aside to examine the incision, but he's lost his taste for her. He doesn't like the way the face muscles have slackened and her skin droops; how the eyes lay open, staring at him. Above those windows to the soul, white muscle and bone shine through.

As he studies his work he sees his mistake. The hole above her brows, slightly off center, not neat enough. Wrong. Or perhaps not wide enough. The pink-beige flecks of brain matter mingle with the blood. Wrong. The incision is also too deep.

Her fault.

She'd moved, even after he'd explained—in detail, always in detail—why she should be still. Usually they listened. Sometimes not. His concentration had wavered and allowed her to move. He grew stronger with each one though, and soon his control would be absolute and he wouldn't need to bind them.

A long sigh escapes his lips. The need remains, tearing again at him like a climax almost there, but fades away. He wanted, *so wanted* for this to be The One.

He sighs again. No matter, he tells himself—even though this does matter—The One is in this city somewhere out there. He senses her like a hum in the air.

He leans over her, the girl he thought, hoped, would open the door to home. From her brow, he wipes a drip of blood, which hangs like dew. Squeezing and smoothing the blood between his fingertips he thinks back to the bus ride. Something is there behind the curtain of his mind. A strange, little catching lingers, scratching at his awareness, crawling into his subconscious, seeking a memory, a very distant memory.

Now hovering there before him.

The redheaded bus driver.

Could this really be him?

What an ironic twist.

Maybe, *maybe,* this one now just blood and bone and empty flesh, is a sign, a glowing flashing marker. Not The One, but fate's message sent for him. He rolls the idea around inside his mind like the last peppermint in a packet, to be savored, considered.

In that slippery, sliding moment, his disappointment begins to heal. If the bus driver has appeared at this moment, this very day, then there *is* a reason. All he needs to discover is why. He'll take his time. He'll watch. Surely the reason will be revealed.

Reasons usually do.

2

*Y*ou could blame what happened on the weather.

If not for the sizzling and humid summer evening, the moisture hanging heavy in the air, clinging to every-one's skin, heralding a storm flying toward us, I might never have done what I did.

Rain or shine, storm or blue skies, everything was all fine by me. The weather might get other people down but never me. I knew better.

"Fine" was a great word.

My wonderful mama used to say: "*Fine* by name—Rory Fine, that is—and *fine* by nature."

She peppered my life with that word from the day I entered this world. Until she drew her last breath, haggard and weary, she still insisted *everything* was fine. Always had been and always would be, no matter how much Adversity knocked at her door she wouldn't allow those bad thoughts in.

According to her, my manners were fine enough for the President, should he ever come to visit. My friends, my quite average school results, my smile, my sandy, red hair—the butt of schoolyard jokes—

my stories, everything, was just fine. Nothing earned her reproach. Nada.

"You're the finest thing in my life," she'd say.

"And you're the finest in mine," I'd reply.

The day she left this earth was certainly Heaven's finest and the saddest day I'll ever live. Her last words, spoken in broken syllables and wisps of sound to me, her sobbing seventeen-year-old who'd kept vigil by her bed hoping for a miracle.

"Don't ... cry, my darling boy. God smiled the day you were born. Have a *fine* life my son. That is your destiny."

She may have revised her prediction if she'd known about this hell-hot day that awaited, nine years down the road. There was too much of what St. Alban folk call the Madness Air. The kind of hot that never helps anyone's mood. Or troubles.

A slight breeze blew in off the Dawson River, trying for all it was worth to cool things down just a little. Without that freshening whisper people'd be crawling up the walls by nightfall. Three days straight the heat had invaded our city and sure made my job all that much harder. At the end of a day, all the passengers wanted was to get to their air-conditioned or fan-cooled homes. You know how people look when they've had enough, their muscles stretched beyond capacity and energy on low flow? Well, this described my passengers today. Every single one of them.

I've been driving buses for five years now. A peculiar job for a young man, I know. I know. At twenty-six I should be exploring the world, making my mark, building some kind of résumé to show I've done something with my life and secured my future.

For me though, this job is perfect fitting like a glove with my other more important work. *Life Job*, as I think of my sideline business.

Probably what I do is a smaller scale version of solving global warming by switching off a single light bulb one lamp at a time. So a big job. *Big*. Yet, one by one, I switched off those bulbs, because who knew the effect that might have? Think of my intervention as saving one butterfly that might flap its wings in Bangkok and, in flapping those little wings averts a bushfire in Australia and saves a town. You know the Butterfly Effect, right? That's me, the Butterfly Effect guy. Except, I call this thing I do troubles keeping, which makes me a Troubles Keeper.

I love this job, both jobs, most days. Looking for greener pastures doesn't enter my mind. Even if those thoughts did, I couldn't leave, because in the last six months all had changed. I simply can't leave until everything plays out.

3

Mariana entered my life via the bus's front boarding steps. She delicately boarded the bus, gliding like a dream. Her smile, followed by a casual "hello," hit me like an electric spark that traveled up my spine and charged my soul. Think those zap things that restart hearts. Her smile did that to me. *Smile. Spark. Zap.* Now I'm magnetized to her. *Nope, I can't leave now.*

I'm in glorious, wonderful, very fine love.

The day she hit me with that warm smile was cold, wet, and nasty; not a day you'd expect love to come a knocking. She climbed aboard my bus, soaked and bedraggled, golden-blonde coils, dark with moisture, poking out from beneath her raincoat hood.

Mariana pushed back the hood of her green-with-pink roses patterned coat, looked down her front, then back at me.

"Sorry. I'm dripping. Raining crazy out there. Am I okay?"

Droplets ran down her jacket to puddle on the charcoal-colored steps as she stared at me through running-mascara-blackened eyes. A gentle, magical light switched on instantly brightening that cloud-darkened day.

I heard my Mama's voice whisper in my ear. *Rory, she's the finest,*

most beautiful natural woman in the world. I like her. I know Mama,
me too.

I remember that day like yesterday, remember I'd wanted to say
something smart, something flirty and light. Normally I'm good with
a quip. Witty Fine, some call me. Something happened to my brain or
my heart or whatever had joyfully twisted inside my chest. My voice
had been suddenly held hostage so the best I had managed was a nod
toward the back of the bus and a limp smile.

"Thank you," she'd said, pulling and pushing at her coat as
though removing a layer of skin. More drops flew about her. Then
she had moved down the aisle, her coat now over her arm. The last
glance I had snatched in my mirror was of her seating herself next to
Mr. Ogilvy (gray-haired, weary eyes and always missing his son).

Six months ago that had happened and still I hadn't worked up
anything close to enough courage to squeak more than a "hello" or
"have a nice day." I guess that's why today I became bold and took a
risk. On reflection, what possessed me?

Love. Unexpressed love.

On this stifling day, air sticky with invisible moisture, the high-
light was my anticipation of Mariana's stop. Nearly two years now, the
nine-zero-five was my regular route, traveling through City Central
with its towering buildings, bustle of shops and department stores,
clutter of lunch bars and cafes, and thousands of workers navigating
the streets, seemingly always in a rush. From the city we enjoyed a
picturesque two-mile drive along the wide and glistening-blue
Dawson River, the focal point of the city. Then, on to East Village
(doesn't every city have an East Village?). Here we passed the
ramshackle, no-longer-in-use, ancient cemetery. Then along
Ellsworth Road, the epicenter of the village, dotted with small
boutiques, sweet, fine eateries nestled beneath low-rise residential
apartment blocks, (sprung up like well-watered saplings since the
reinvigoration of the area).

The route terminated at East Village train station by Benedict
House, so named to conceal the building was really a halfway house

for addicts on the mend. Then the route reversed back the same way. Three hours after I'd swung the bus out the gates, I drove back into the depot for a break, before repeating the journey all over again.

What most people would consider a mundane job—same streets, same view, same stops and starts—I enlivened by getting to know my regulars. In fact, I did more than get to know them, more than transport them from A to B. I helped them. I changed lives.

They never understood, of course, why on the odd occasion their commute left them happier, more content than when they'd boarded. Maybe they thought the change in mood was due to my friendly smile, or the chance to relax while someone else drove, or that anywhere was better than where they'd just left.

But the difference was me. My touch. My gift to them, delivered without a trace, without a sound, without anybody knowing why suddenly the world seemed a brighter place; the troubles they carried when they left their homes that morning now not so heavy.

I didn't need a thank you or to leave a florist's calling card: *Here's a gift because I can, because I want to make the world a better place.* I didn't need acknowledgment; all I needed were their smiles, their improved moods, and to see extra bounce in their steps as though they no longer toted that emotional backpack.

Troubles. They stick to skin like glue, like gum to the sole of a shoe. They slide into the crevices of your heart, slither into your veins, and tug at you from the inside until they become something dark and heavy and not so easy to shake.

The length of time you allow them to take up residence, that's what makes all the difference between the good, the bad, and the ugly days. Sure, you can brush them aside—and most good folk usually do—but what gets you is the sometimes; the sometimes when shrugging off troubles may not be so simple.

I took away the sometimes.

Dawson River was my favorite stretch. Some days the word *fine* just wasn't enough. The sun rising, yellow and pink, a present to those awake, and the sun setting over glistening water, warm gold, a splendid vista that made you believe in all things good. Some days the river didn't need the sun to shine. Rain splashing its surface, urged small white-tipped waves to rise up like dancing handker-chiefs. I knew this river like a friend. We shared a secret; in fact, we were allies.

This five-fourteen afternoon run was my favorite. Not just because of Mariana, either. My best work was done in these hours. If people ever needed relief from their troubles, the time was after a hard day's work. But, for whatever reason on that day, most passen-gers seemed to feel the weight of life more than usual. I guess that's why I did what I did, before I'd thought the whole thing through.

4

*H*e peers through the bus window at the ominous clouds. The light drops of rain, quickly turn the gray of the sidewalk to a mottled black. He likes this dark brand of sky. People are less aware, far more concerned with getting to shelter, staying dry, worrying about plans made more difficult by the heavens spilling down.

Though he walks freely among them, beside these scurrying creatures of habit, there's always a risk he'll be recognized for his true self. Rain feels like an invisible cloak; the humidity like soft, protective fiber against his skin.

Until he found *him* on this bus in the late afternoon, he had spent the day traveling the bus routes, attempting to ascertain if what he felt yesterday was because of this bus, or this man, or a random connection to something else. *Now he knows.* He'd moved seats numerous times, reached out and brushed a few of those around him. *Nothing.* Just a nagging frustration growing within that he may have been mistaken.

Now as he watches him—yes, and the man *is* him—he understands like a faded memory reinvigorated by an old song or the whiff of an intangible scent. He *knows* his search is over.

With each stop he studies the driver, cobbles his memories together, and wonders why he hadn't sought him out before. Of course, he may help him to open the door. *Friend or enemy, though?*

The way he looks at the girl, all golden hair and a smile, as she climbs aboard and skims past the driver, reveals so much. This makes perfect sense; the two of them special lights in a world filled with half-opened doorways and empty rooms. They are both of the same design.

As she maneuvers down the aisle, the girl places a hand on the seat back in front of him. He reaches out nonchalantly to touch her. Electric fire, blue and sharp, rushes through his skin.

She could be The One.

He soaks in this knowledge, and the peace this thought brings. This long search could be over. Her brow lifts playfully as she looks down at his hand; surprise crosses her face. He smiles and withdraws the hand, feigning embarrassment. She smiles. Unsuspecting. No reason to fear. A random accident of physicality, a moving bus, an unbalanced body.

Now she is his and he can source her at will. A thrill plays through him and goosebumps rise on his skin. For the next fifteen minutes he slides between exhilaration and frustration that he must wait until tonight. He'll follow, but he's learned through experience that timing is everything.

Then the bus stops and the driver stands facing down the aisle. He introduces himself. *Rory Fine.* Has the man recognized him? Surely the bus driver cannot know or he would have noticed a reaction.

As the bus driver talks he begins to understand. This isn't a random chance meeting that he is here on this bus with her. Something grander is at play. He just needs to figure out exactly what that means.

Continue reading

The Troubles Keeper

Read for FREE with Kindle Unlimited or Kindle Prime

ALSO BY SUSAN MAY

NOVELS

The Goodbye Giver (The Troubles Keeper 2)

(coming July 2019)

Best Seller

The Troubles Keeper

Back Again

Deadly Messengers

NOVELLA

Behind the Fire

291

(coming February 2019)

OMNIBUS

Happy Nightmares! Thriller Omnibus

SHORT STORY COLLECTIONS

Destination Dark Zone

(coming March 2019)

Behind Dark Doors (one)

Behind Dark Doors (two)

Behind Dark Doors (three)

Behind Dark Doors (the complete collection)

(Includes one, two and three)

WHISPERSYNC AUDIBLE NARRATION

Best Seller

Back Again

Deadly Messengers

The Troubles Keeper

THE TROUBLES KEEPER
BY SUSAN MAY
Copyright 2016 Susan May

All stories in this volume
BY SUSAN MAY
Copyright 2010-2015 Susan May

❀ Created with Vellum

CPSIA information can be obtained
at www.ICGtesting.com
Printed in the USA
LVHW111004290719
625700LV00001B/120/P